This is a work of fiction. Names, characters, places and incidents either are the product of the author's imagination or used fictitiously. Any resemblance to actual persons living or dead, events, or locales is entirely coincidental.

Cover Design from CANVA

For Wen.
I know you would have loved these.

Special thanks to my partner, Jay Dax, for editing these monologues and helping me with the Bo'ness accent in *Dreams O' New York.*

Foreword

These monologues are written to be performed, and are therefore punctuated accordingly – with commas, dashes and full stops indicating different lengths of breath. For best results, read out loud and, if possible, in the accent intended.

When it is safe to do so, I hope to both film these monologues and record them as podcasts. Royalties from this book will be used to hire professional actresses and crew to make this happen.

Thank you very much for your support.

Rachel Dax

Dear Siân

I hope you enjoy these 'boring' monologues! :)

Love and best wishes

Rachel Dax

xxx

IN ISOLATION

By Rachel Dax

Contents

Monologue 1. ***Dreams O' New York***

Monologue 2. ***Dressed For Men***

Monologue 3. ***People Like Us***

Monologue 4. ***Footballer's Wife***

Monologue 1.

Dreams O' New York

[MARY, AGED EIGHTY, IS SITTING IN A SMALL GARDEN OUTSIDE A 1970s PEBBLE-DASHED 'SCOTTISH SPECIAL' HOUSE. SHE IS WEARING A SMART BUT INEXPENSIVE OUTFIT OF GREEN AND BLUE TARTAN TROUSERS, WHITE NYLON BLOUSE, DARK GREEN COTTON CARDIGAN AND FLAT, BLACK SLIP-ON SHOES. SHE SPEAKS WITH A STRONG BO'NESS ACCENT.]

I fell in love for the first time at the age o' seventy. 'Seventy?' you cry. I ken. It does sound daft – a woman like me wi' four weans and nine grandweans – never been in love, not even as a lassie, and then suddenly – BANG – oot o' nowhere, running around like a teenager again. Dear God, the last ten years have been amazing, I tell you. I didnae ken that happiness like this existed.

I hear you. I do. Asking, 'What? How? Why?'
But first I need to say that there are others… Like me… Who had dozens o' fellas but never fell in love.
Aw… you want to ken aboot the fellas? Well I'm no stranger to the cock. That's for sure.

Ok, let me go back to the beginning. I grew up in a town called Bo'ness. Halfway between Glasgow and Edinburgh, on the Firth O' Forth – you ken – where the Forth Rail Bridge is. That bit. Ma dad worked down the pit, and ma mam in our wee house scrubbing away all day. I was the youngest one o' nine. Pape not Prod – so aboot an average sized family – given I was born in 1940.

Well, I left school at fourteen – back then you could if you were a lassie. And I wasnae much good at any o' it anyways. I kent what fate had in store for me. Leave school, work for a few years, get married, have eight or ten weans, become a granny and if lucky, a great granny… and then die. Why did I need an education? Ma life was mapped oot for me from the moment ma own granny cried down from the bedroom to ma father, 'It's a girl!'

So at fourteen, I started a job in the shirt factory, where most o' the young women o' the town would work until they got married, and then maybe come back again as old girls if their husband had died and the weans were grown.

It didnae take long for me to ken I wasn't suited to being in a factory full o' women all day. 'Are you winching yet, hen?' they'd ask me constantly – for those o' you who dinnae speak Scottish that means, 'Do you have a boyfriend?' All day, every day, women everywhere talking aboot what women back then talked aboot – boys, men, husbands, clothes, singers they wanted to kiss and film stars they wanted to marry. I hated it. I hated everything aboot it and I made up ma mind to go and work somewhere else… wi' men. At least then I might have an answer to, 'Are you winching, hen?' or 'Have you got a steady fella yet, Mary?'

So after six months o' torture, being surrounded by women, I got maself a job at the brewery. And now there were men everywhere. All ages, heights, looks. Plenty o' young ones near ma age too. It took a certain type o' man to work at the brewery rather than down the pit. The miners, like ma father, were gruff and grimy and on the whole drank half their wages down the pub every night. But funnily enough the brewery men, although surrounded by beer all day, tended to drink less and generally were very clean. I mean – maybe they smelled a bit o' hops – but their hands were scrubbed and they didnae have black coal dust embedded in every crease and cranny. There wasnae hand sanitiser back then, just plenty o' soap and water. Believe it or not, ma generation didnae need Corona Virus to remind us to wash our hands. But anyways, mostly they were men a girl would want to be around.

I liked working in the brewery. Ma job was to wash the returned bottles – we kent aboot recycling back then too. Empty bottles were returned and you got a penny for your trouble. All the pop was in bottles too – none o' this plastic shite that's causing all the problems now.

Sorry, I digress… I was young, and pretty and surrounded by men and o' course, I was asked oot on dates. But I wasnae even fifteen yet, so I would say, 'Naw, thank you.' After all, I had strict Catholic parents.

But soon there was an expectation. Older sisters first, then aunties and then eventually ma mother, every other week the same question: 'Are you winching yet, hen?' To which the answer was always 'naw'. Gradually, sorry smiles turned to judgements and I kent I had to do something to appease the nagging banshees that constantly bombarded me wi' this same question.

So I decided to put a stop to it. I hadnae taken a fancy to anyone at the brewery, clean and pleasant though most o' the young men were. But a laddie called Alfie had been sweet on me for a while and so I decided to sit next to him in the yard and eat ma lunch piece wi' him. He asked me on a date and I said I might do one day but I wanted to get to ken him a bit better first. So we started sitting on the wall eating our pieces every day. A few weeks later, he asked me oot again and I said 'naw' then as well. He looked sad but said, 'Well can we meet behind the big vat tomorrow? Because there's something I want to say to you in private.' I kent this meant he wanted to kiss me and I thought, 'Well ok. That'll be safer than goin' to a dance.'

You have to remember that back then young lassies had to walk a tightrope between being available to men for winching but not getting pregnant. If you weren't available you were frigid... and if you were too available you were a slut... You were maybe allowed a few boyfriends before settling down but too many and you were a hussy or much too fussy. It was a balancing act that so many lassies fell foul o'. If you got pregnant before getting hitched, you were the scandal o' the town. Naebody, literally naebody would speak to you. You couldnae go to the Chapel. You couldnae get it 'seen to' wi'oot burning in Hell. Ach, it was hard on lassies back then. So many ended up in some kind o' misery because they got it wrong. Sent away to a home for unmarried mothers or married off quickly and sent to another town so naebody would ken the timeline. Poor cows, the lot o' them.

I didnae want to live in misery. But I also didnae want ma sisters, aunties, mother, cousins and neighbours on at me all the time either. So I decided this was the way to manage it. I'd meet Alfie behind the large vat at lunchtime – naebody would be there as everybody had their lunch at twelve. And I'd let him kiss me.

And that's how it started... I let him kiss me. I felt nothing but he seemed to like it and said thank you. After that, I met him behind the vat every lunchtime. And we'd kiss and kiss some more. Each time he would try and touch me a bit but because I didnae fancy him, I didnae really like it – so I'd push him away. Kissing a man you arenae in love wi' is enough.

He'd always try for more. I'd always refuse. Then one day, he got cross and said, 'I'm goin' to tell all the fellas here you're frigid.' At which point, I panicked and for ma own survival, I put ma hand on his trousers where he was already bulging and I took oot his cock and I rubbed it until he spilled oot all over the floor. Afterwards, he smiled, his eyes were wide and he was shuddering. I said, 'I'm not frigid. I just cannae have a wean before I wed and one thing can lead to another so I'd rather just touch you and you dinnae touch me. Have we a deal?' And he grinned and said, 'You mean you'd do that for me again, Mary?' And I nodded and said, 'Aye. Every day. So long as you dinnae put your hands on me.' And I kissed him then and let him mop up his mess wi' his handkerchief.

And that's how it went on. Naebody kent – there was nae such thing as CCTV back then and I guess they just assumed that because we were winching, we'd gone oot for a walk.

I wanked Alfie off behind the beer vats for over a year wi'oot goin' on a single date. When the cry o', 'Are you winching yet, hen?' came I'd say, 'Aye, his name is Alfie and we walk oot together every lunchtime.' And that seemed to keep everybody happy until I was sixteen…

But something funny used to happen once you turned sixteen. You couldnae refuse dates to young folks' dances or the pictures anymore. You couldnae because now it was expected. Alfie began to nag. But I just didnae want to. And then, inevitably I suppose, he turned around to me one day and said, 'Wee Ginger who works in the office says she'll go wi' me to the dance at the Chapel hall on Saturday night. Do you mind?' And I said, 'Naw, go ahead.' It didnae take long before he was having his lunch piece wi' Ginger instead o' me but I really didnae mind. I was never goin' to fall in love wi' him and he was never really in love wi' me – at least he never told me he was, however much I rubbed his cock. So I was happy he'd found somebody else.

But o' course, now I wasnae winching anymore and I couldnae lie aboot Alfie because Bo'ness is a small town and it wouldnae take long to be found oot. So I gave it a few weeks until the pressure aboot being single at nearly seventeen years o' age became too much, and then a laddie called John started asking me on dates. I agreed to sit wi' him at lunch so we could get to ken each other better. And then, wi'in a couple o' weeks, when he started nagging to go to the Chapel dance, I said, 'I will, eventually, but let's have our first kiss somewhere naebody can see us.' Then I took him behind the big vats and before long, it was just the same wi' him – after a few times kissing, he started to fumble and fiddle wi' ma clothes and I, again, not remotely in love and not wanting to be touched, reached down to his trousers and started rubbing his cock. And there we were.

'Are you winching, again, hen?' asked Mammy.
'Aye – wi' John McManners – you ken – Maggie and Jimmy's son. We have a walk every lunchtime.'
'Ach Mary, you dinnae think you should be doing a bit more than having a walk? Why di you naw go to the dance down at the Chapel, like your sisters did?'
'Aye – I will, Mam, soon enough.'
She looked at me in a way that only a mother could look at a daughter and tell her everything she needed to ken wi'oot saying a word. A shudder o' fear ran through me.
'Aye, Mam. I was planning on goin' to the one at the end o' the month.'

I went to the dance wi' John. And we had plenty o' fun dancing. Then afterwards, he walked me home via the woods. I rubbed him til he was done and then he looked at me and said, 'You're never goin' to let me touch you, are you, Mary?' And I said, 'Naw. I dinnae want a wean until I'm wed.' Then he said, 'But you dinnae want to marry me do you?' And I looked down at ma shoes and said, 'You should marry a girl you're in love wi' and who's in love wi' you, John McManners and both o' us ken that isnae me.'

We didnae meet again behind the vat. But after him came Mark, then Billy and then Russell. All at the brewery, all happy for me to wank them off at lunchtime and after the Chapel dance on Saturday nights – until someone who wanted more than me came along. None o' them ever seemed to hate me for not loving them but like wi' all men, once something stops, you dinnae stay pals. So that would be that. Nae more chat. Nae more smiles. As if nothing had happened in the first place.

I was nineteen now. And ma mammy sat me down and said, 'Hen. You need to think aboot saying 'I do' to one o' these fellas you go dancing wi', or folk are goin' to talk. You arenae sixteen anymore. People will be thinking you're a slapper if you carry on like this wi' a new laddie every six months. And if they dinnae think you're a slapper, they'll be thinking there's something wrong wi' you – that a fella cannae stand you for long enough to pop the question.' I nodded. Kenning she was right. I had to get engaged next time or there'd be nothing but trouble down the road.

It was around that time that a young woman ma age called Lottie, started working in the brewery. There wernae many women working there and I was the only one in ma section. She was employed as a bottle labeller, and worked the other side o' the floor from me. She was engaged to a fella called Max who worked in Falkirk as a fishmonger. She was a friendly lassie and always stopped for a chat. She had bright blue eyes and a mass o' curly blond hair that fell oot o' her cloth hat. I was between fellas so took to sitting wi' her at lunchtimes and we talked aboot the pictures and music and where we would go if we had money to ever travel. I told her the only place I dreamed o' goin' was New York – I'd seen it in a hundred films and thought it must be the most exciting place on earth, and she agreed.

She was easy company and we laughed a lot. Then one morning she said, 'Come to the disused lassies changing room down by the gate at lunchtime. I've got something I want to show you.' There was part o' me that kent this wasnae right because alarm bells started ringing in ma head as soon as she asked. But I agreed, anyways, not wanting to hurt her feelings if she had a secret to tell.

So that lunchtime, as requested, I went to the old changing room, and when I got there she was waiting. The light didnae work, she told me – so it was dim from just one wee high window. She looked at me and said, 'Mary, I…' and then wi'oot further ado, she stepped forward and kissed me on the lips. I kent that what she wanted was immoral. I'd never heard the word 'lesbian' back then. But naebody had to tell me it was wrong because a few years before, there'd been two fellas who'd been sent to jail for being caught at it in the bushes down by the foreshore. It had been the scandal o' the town for months. I pulled back and looked at her horrified, fear racing through me – making me almost dizzy – then I slapped her hard across the face and ran oot o' there, not looking back.

I went back to work that afternoon but I couldnae concentrate and managed to smash at least half a dozen bottles, making the foreman furious. I refused to even look in the direction o' Lottie's workstation and left on the first ring o' the bell.

On ma way home, I walked straight to the engine factory three miles down the road and asked them if they had any jobs goin'. The manager looked me up and down and said that the men would be delighted to have a bonnie lassie like me serving them in the canteen and asked if I could start on Monday, to which I said, 'Aye'. The next morning, which was a Friday, I went into the brewery as usual but told ma boss that I wouldnae be back. I asked him not to say anything to the staff as I didnae want any fuss. There was nae sign o' Lottie and I didnae ask why she hadnae come to work that day. Because I kent. She kent what she'd done was a sin, and that if I told anybody she'd be hounded oot o' both home and town. I was so appalled by what had happened, I vowed never to even think aboot it again and I pushed it oot o' ma mind.

I had a new job. A new factory full o' men. I was nineteen years old and I needed to find a husband.

You cannae meet laddies at lunchtime if you work in a canteen. And at nineteen, nearly twenty, you were expected to do more than just go dancing or to the pictures once a week. That was for young folk finding their feet. If you were female, twenty and not at least engaged, there was nothing but comment. 'You dinnae want to be left on the shelf, hen.'... 'You're too fussy, lassie.'… 'If you keep turning these fellas down you'll end up a spinster.' And so it went.

It was at the engine factory that I had ma first bad encounter wi' a fella. I'd worked wi' men for over four years and apart from the odd wolf whistle and a pinch on the arse, I'd never had any bother. But at the engine factory, the men were a bit rougher and a bit gobbier. If a lassie didnae have a fella, or in some cases didnae have a fella at that factory, then she could be in trouble. Nae such thing as 'Women's Lib' back then. If a girl protested, she could be ruined wi' a few choice words. If a girl caved in, then she had to make sure she only caved enough to get oot the other side in one piece. As I said, I was planning to get engaged to the next nice laddie that asked anyways. But after a big bastard called Douglas followed me home from work and tried to drag me into the woods, I kent I couldnae wait. I got away from Douglas but I never went home that way again. It was too easy for a man like that to pull a girl in on a dark winter's night and naebody would believe a word she said – even if she came home covered in blood. There wasnae any 'Me Too' back then either. If you were the woman, then you always lost. It was always your own fault. Nae matter what. 'Well, what was she doing near the woods at that time o' night?' or 'Well, have you seen the length o' her skirt?' or 'Well, she's had so many boyfriends, he probably thought she wanted it.' You didnae stand a chance.

Anyways, Hamish, who also worked at the factory, had smiled at me a few times while I served him his grub. And I kent he was single because he was ma cousin's best friend. A year older than me, wi' a steady attitude, he seemed right enough. So when he waited at the factory gate one night and asked if he could walk me home, I let him. I was twenty, he was twenty-one. He'd been engaged to a lassie for a while but her family had moved to Canada, and she didnae want to be left behind and he didnae want to go – so they'd broken it off.

It didnae take long for Hamish to be wanting more than just a kiss. And being older, finding excuses was more difficult. So wi'in a couple o' dates, I was satisfying him in the woods or in his dad's garden shed. Until one night, I saw a glint in his eye and he pushed me hard against the wall and started pulling roughly at ma clothes. I was terrified. I hadnae expected it and I thought we had an arrangement but naw, he said he'd been patient enough. You ken, it's funny. What you remember – and when and how you use it for your survival. I kent I wasnae goin' to get oot o' that shed unless he got more than a hand around his cock. And as he started being even more forceful, I remembered ma sister telling me what a boyfriend, who was a sailor, had asked her to do to him wi' her mouth – because that's how they did it in France – but she'd refused. 'Hamish,' I hissed. 'Wait. I have another way – one where I won't get knocked up.' He still didnae stop but I tugged at him and said, 'Let me show you first and then if you dinnae like it, I promise we can try the other.' The glint was still in his eye but he hesitated, so I quickly went down on ma knees and showed him exactly what I meant. Being a typical man o' his time, he had no idea such things existed and wi'in moments was ecstatic and loud enough to disturb the neighbours. Afterwards, he said, 'I'm sorry Mary. I ken I pushed you too far for the other. But if we do this every night from now on, I won't push again.' I nodded and left. And then broke up wi' him the next day at the factory gates.

Why am I telling you all this, you ask? Why do I need to tell you aboot how I learned to suck cock? Well in all honesty, it meant that I had a happy marriage. After Hamish, I was on ma last chance wi' ma mother. She was furious that I'd let another 'decent man' go and was getting a reputation for giving men the run around. I kent more than ever that I had to marry ma next fella. I was yet to feel a *single* loving emotion, even though I was now nearly twenty-one and had rubbed more cock in the last six years than most women have in a lifetime. When I met David at ma second cousin's wedding, and he asked me to dance, I kent he was somebody I should seriously consider. He was a painter on the Forth Rail Bridge – so he would never be oot o' work. Ma parents kent and liked his family. He was twenty-two, single and seemed good-natured. So we started winching. I told him flat oot that I wouldnae let any man touch me until ma wedding night, but there were things I could do for him that would make him happy. For the first few weeks he was happy wi' ma hand and then, when he started getting restless, I gave him ma mouth and afterwards, he asked me to marry him. I said yes. But again, told him I wouldnae do any more until our wedding night. He smiled and said that what we'd just done made him feel like we'd got married anyways, and he'd be more than happy to wait. And he was. He was a nice man. Simple. He liked his job. He didnae drink heavily. He played amateur football on Saturdays and went fishing all day Sundays. I kent that even if it wasnae all hearts and flowers, I could tolerate him. So a year later, I stopped the nagging voices once and for all, and I married him.

It's hard to believe now, after all this talk o' cock that I was a virgin on ma wedding night. But I assure you, I was. Naebody had even succeeded in taking ma bra off. I didnae want him inside me but I kent I had nae choice. So I lay back and thought o'… naw… not England. Why would I want to think o' the land o' the Sassenach? I lay back and thought o' Grangemouth Oil Refinery. I ken, I ken – but not the version o' the oil refinery you see in the day, but how it looks at night – all lit up in the dark – like the twinkling New York City skyline. The only place I had ever dreamed o' goin'. It hurt and I didnae enjoy it. But I kent that as long as I let him do it to me now and again, and the rest o' the time I did the other two things I was so expert at by now, then he would be happy enough and I could stand it. Besides, we'd agreed to wait a bit before having weans because it would be nice to buy our own wee flat – and if we saved enough, we could move oot o' his parents' house where we were living until the Council had a place for us.

And so for aboot a year and a half, that's what we did. I kept him happy and kept maself as happy as I could be – given I wasnae remotely in love and was goin' to be wi' him for the rest o' ma life. He didnae notice I wasnae in love. Like a lot o' men o' his generation, he didnae talk aboot emotions. He'd only told me he loved me a couple o' times and I'd replied 'me too' rather than saying the words themselves, and he hadnae even clocked it. I made good food, caused no trouble and we got on well enough to have a wee laugh now and again.

It was the least harassed I'd been by ma family since the age o' sixteen. Nae more, 'Are you winching, hen?' Nae more, 'Why aren't you married yet, lassie – you'll end up on the shelf.' But then, as I said, aboot eighteen months on, it started: 'Are you naw pregnant yet, Mary?' ma father would ask. 'Is everything goin' alright in the bedroom department?' ma mam would whisper, disappointed to see ma stomach still flat.

And so it began… Drip, drip, drip… until it was a deluge o' sisters, cousins and neighbours. Naebody ever asked me whether I actually wanted any weans. Naebody even thinks to ask a working class woman that question. And besides, even all the middle class women back then had weans unless they were a dreaded spinster or a nun. If anybody, including David, had actually asked me what I wanted rather than assumed, I would have said, 'naw' but o' course naebody did. And then one night David sat me down and said, 'I can't go on saving for a house before we have weans, Mary. The laddies at work keep taking the piss. Saying I cannae get it up or saying I'm firing blanks.' I remember looking at him and deciding whether to argue or not. Tell him that I didnae really want weans… but I hadnae told him before we got married, I'd let him assume I did. So I couldnae turn around now and say that. We never argued and I wanted it to stay that way. So I took a deep breath and said, 'Aye. I'm getting it too. Maybe we could just have the one and then keep saving like we planned. It'll take a year or two longer but they'll give us a council house if I'm pregnant and at least it'll be a place o' our own.'

O' course, we never did have enough to buy our own place. Because once we had one baby, wi'in eighteen months there was pressure to have another, and then another, and then more. It wasnae until I nearly died after having ma fourth that finally the nagging stopped and ma family, his family and the rest o' Bo'ness were satisfied enough to leave us alone. By that time, I wasnae working any longer and his wages just aboot covered the bills. Nae home o' our own. Another dream, like goin' to New York, that was never, ever goin' to happen.

I ken, I ken, I've talked for ages but I still havnae told you aboot how I finally, unexpectedly fell in love and you've become impatient. So I'll cut to the chase…

David and I were together until he died o' a heart attack aged fifty-two. By which time, I was already a granny twice over. I was sad when he died. He'd been a good husband and we'd got on well. He'd never once hit me. He'd never been unkind. And he was oot o' the house enough not to annoy me to excess. After he went, I missed him.

Here's the thing. And I must tell you this. Once you pass child-bearing age and especially once you're a granny, naebody has any sexual expectations o' you as a woman ever again. Naebody. Naebody starts asking, 'Are you winching, hen?' When you're in your fifties, they leave you alone. When you go back to work part time, naebody pinches your arse or asks you to dances. You're invisible. You're nothing. You dinnae exist in any real way at all.

I loved ma weans in spite o' never wanting any. I loved ma grandweans just as much. I had pleased everybody eventually. Naebody had any great reason to be disappointed wi' me. Even ma mother, in the end, thought I'd done a grand job o' ma life.

So I drifted. Drifted in a way only a woman o' that age could. Working part-time in the school canteen. Baby sitting the grandweans. Watching TV when I was on ma own.

I had nae friends. I dinnae ken whether you noticed that before. That I had nae friends. I'd avoided it. I'd just stuck wi' ma family, feeling it was… safer.

But then… and this is the bit you want to ken aboot, isn't it? Who is he? Who is the man I finally fell in love wi' aged seventy…?

Well… Remember how I told you I'd always dreamed o' goin' to New York. And back then it *was* a dream. Only rich people went to places like that. You have to remember that I was in ma forties before working class people even started goin' to Torremolinos for their holidays – it's only nowadays that people like me can even think o' goin' to America. Abroad wasnae something that we did.

But, anyways, ma three daughters and ma son kent I'd always wanted to go to New York, and like so many o' their generation, they had a better education and better paying jobs than me or David could ever have hoped for. So they decided to treat me to a week in the city o' ma dreams.

It was at the airport that I fell in love. I was excited. Ma guard was down. Finally I would see the Big Apple for real, not just in a film. I couldnae wait. It was only ma second time abroad. I'd been to Majorca for ma sixtieth wi' ma eldest and her weans – that was it.

Anyways…

[MARY TAKES A DEEP BREATH]

This is the bit you've been waiting for... I was in Glasgow Airport at the boarding gate, looking around at the other travellers when I noticed a familiar face staring across at me. You have to realise that time ravages a woman's looks so it can take a wee while to work oot who a person is. And then, when I did, I was filled wi' a tingling rush so powerful that I felt all giddy. I didnae think to stop maself. I didnae hesitate for a moment. I simply got up oot o' ma seat and walked over.

There was naebody else those big blue eyes could belong to but her. Lottie. The lassie who'd kissed me over fifty years ago. The lassie I'd slapped and then run away from. She was there wi' her twin sons. She stood up and we gave each other a hug. And said all the usual things like, 'I cannae believe it's you!' and, 'I havnae seen you since we were lassies.' And then, we pulled back, wi' hands still holding our elbows and gave each other a look. The kind o' look that can pass between two women and say everything wi'oot anyone else seeing a thing. In that look, I kent that I was the only girl she'd ever tried to kiss. That she, like me, had married a man she didnae love, had settled and had conformed. And I also kent that this time, if she kissed me, I wouldnae run. I wouldnae disappear. I wouldnae push the incident so far down inside o' me that it was like it never happened. I would kiss her back. By now the rush o' love was so overwhelming that I thought I might give maself away, but I looked around and everybody was smiling. 'Two old women, who were friends when they were but wee lassies, bumping into each other at the airport. How lovely.'

And so I looked at her and asked her the very thing I kent she wanted to hear from ma lips, 'Would you like to meet up and go somewhere together when we're both in New York?' Her eyes lit up and her smile was broad. 'Aye. I'd love to. How aboot The Statue O' Liberty?' she replied. It couldnae have been anywhere else really, could it? Because we kent. Not just me. We both kent already that we were finally free. Phone numbers were exchanged, plans arranged. I went back to ma seat. And tried not to look at her constantly.

For the first time in ma life, I was falling in love. Really falling in love. When we got on the plane, she was at the other end from me – so we didnae really see each other during the flight. But I kent she'd be fidgeting in her seat – wanting to be wi' me as much as me wi' her. I couldnae manage normal conversation so I pretended to be asleep and thought back to when I was young.

I told you earlier. I never really had any friends. But I didnae tell you why. I'd never admitted to maself that the reason why I didnae fancy or love those men was because I liked women. That thought – not even the thought that might have come before it – was never allowed to form in ma head. Naw. It was so pushed down, so repressed that I never, ever said to maself, 'I fancy that lassie – what's wrong wi' me?' Or, 'I think I'm falling in love wi' that woman.' Naw. Instead, I avoided women. Somehow kenning they were dangerous for me.

When I looked back, I realised it was why I left the shirt factory before I turned fifteen. I wasnae like the other women there. I couldnae participate in their conversations because I didnae feel the things they felt or think the things they thought aboot men. And I think – it's so long ago now, it's hard to say for sure – that I must have started to notice them. Not all o' them. But maybe one or two. The way they smiled or laughed perhaps excited me a wee bit too much. A glance too long as they leaned over in a certain way. I think maybe I started to feel desire and so I made maself stop before I even acknowledged what it meant. Far safer to flee to the world o' men. Surround maself wi' men. Rub cock after cock. Suck cock and then eventually lie back and think o' Grangemouth. Naebody could ever doubt that I liked a good man. I had more boyfriends than any o' ma sisters, cousins or neighbours' daughters. Naebody could suspect for a moment that I didnae love or fancy a single one o' them. Except perhaps ma mother… Remember the look I told you aboot? It was that look when I kent that *she kent* there was something wrong wi' me… even if she didnae have a name for it. She kent there was *something*, and that I needed to conform. And she wouldnae be happy until I conformed. So I did.

I surrounded maself wi' family. Only went oot wi' family. And remained a distantly polite neighbour. All wi'oot giving the reason why a name. In later years, as these things began being talked aboot and even shown on TV, I always found a way to avoid the conversation, turn over the drama where the women were falling in love, before they kissed. Always stopped it. Halted it. Denied maself it. I couldnae. Wouldnae. Shouldnae.

But then, there on the aeroplane, I let maself use the word. The L word. LESBIAN. 'I am a lesbian.' I found maself saying in ma head. 'I am a lesbian and I am goin' to kiss Lottie… and make love wi' her in New York... I am a lesbian and I am goin' to let maself fall head over heals in love. I am a lesbian and I have always been a lesbian and nae amount o' sucked cock can change it.'

On our third day there, we met at the ferry terminal and went to The Statue O' Liberty as planned. We sat close, wi' the backs o' our hands touching. Fidgeting in our seats, chattering away aboot our lives but wanting to do nothing but caress and kiss. When we got to The Statue O' Liberty, tears began rolling down ma cheeks because I really felt I was being liberated. Somehow, we managed to climb to the very top despite our arthritic knees. And when we stood looking oot o' the great lady, at the spectacular view, I turned to Lottie and kissed her on the cheek, and whispered, 'Is it safe to go to your hotel room?' I was sharing a room wi' ma youngest daughter, so there was nae chance o' anything happening there. 'Aye,' she replied. 'Let's get the next boat back.'

We made love that afternoon like two teenagers. The two teenagers we were when we met. I didnae need to lie back and think o' Grangemouth Oil Refinery at night. I was in the real New York. Feeling real love and real desire. I was in the land o' the free and the city where dreams are made. I loved the feel o' her touch. I didnae need to service her to avoid being groped by an undesired hand. I let her explore every inch o' me and revelled in every moment. I had ma first ever orgasm and then ma second and then several more before I left. And so did she. That lassie who'd been brave enough to kiss me at the brewery back in 1961, had lived a life twelve miles up the road that was practically the same as mine. She'd married Max a few months after I ran off. She'd had five weans. Naebody had ever kent. She'd made herself forget... But then there we were. And suddenly nae time had passed at all, and we were as we should've been… and as we would be from now on, until one o' us died.

And we were. We never had a day when we didnae see each other after that. For the first year, we lived between our two houses and then, eventually, we said 'fuck it' and told our families and I moved into her place. Our weans were all shocked, but o' course, it was the twenty-first century by now and gay people were getting married every day o' the week. People were goin' on marches – and with their straight friends too. So naebody really objected or played a face.

I can see you welling up now, because you've realised Lottie has died. Don't cry. Please. This is a happy ending. Lottie and I made love every day for nearly ten years. We were deliriously happy and laughed and giggled and played like the wee lassies we were when we met. O' course, I am broken hearted that she's gone. But I ken how lucky I was to have her. To have had any happiness at all. If I hadnae gone to New York, and gone on that *particular* day, I would've never met her again. I would've spent the last ten years drifting into old age, still living like an empty shell. But instead, I had the richest, most beautiful time o' ma life.

I loved. And I lived. How many people, hand on heart, can say they had ten years o' absolute bliss wi' another human being? So dinnae be sad. Think o' all the women like me who never had this. Who lived and died, never having a chance to be themselves. Think o' all the women living in foreign countries where it's as impossible for them now as it was for me back then.

Think aboot your granny. Do you ken for sure she was happy?

Dinnae be sad. I had a happy ending.

Monologue 2.

Dressed For Men

[SARA, AGED 85, IS SITTING ON THE BALCONY OF A LONDON FLAT WITH THE CITYSCAPE BEHIND HER. SHE IS WEARING A GOOD QUALITY PURPLE COTTON JUMPER, BLACK WOOLLEN TROUSERS AND BLACK MOCCASIN SHOES. SHE SPEAKS WITH A MIDDLE CLASS SWANSEA ACCENT.]

I fell in love with Jack immediately. Some people don't believe that love at first sight is possible but I can honestly tell you, I saw him and I knew he was 'the one'! I was twenty and had not long qualified as a primary school teacher, specialising in music, and I was also already assistant choir mistress at the local Methodist church. One summer's evening on my way home from school, I popped into meet the new church organist and choir master before Sunday services. As I walked into the church twenty minutes early, I was transported to the heavens by the most sublime rendition of Widor's Toccata I had ever heard. Notes resounding from pillar to pillar, floor to vaulted ceiling. The blond haired young man responsible for this celestial performance appeared lost in a wild dream and I stood watching him fascinated, completely transfixed. When the last note faded, I found myself spontaneously applauding and he turned around and looked down on me, grinning from ear to ear. At which point, my heart exploded in my chest.

He climbed down from the organ loft, greeting me excitedly, ‘You must be Sara who plays piano, violin and sings! I’ve been aching to meet you!’ And with that, we started a conversation about music which I knew would never end. As well as being employed by our church, he was also a peripatetic clarinet teacher at High Schools across Swansea. He was the same height as me with cobalt blue eyes and an aquiline nose. Slender but not scrawny. And utterly captivating in every way.

Within a few weeks, Jack and I were inseparable. Each night after work, we would meet in the church hall to arrange hymns for the choir and take it in turns to play the piano whilst the other sang. Afterwards, we would go to the local pub where he would drink port and I sherry. Though he was from the other side of town, Swansea was still small enough in the 1950s for everyone to have a meaningful connection to someone else, and it turned out that Jack taught clarinet at the school where my father was Headmaster. So soon he was treated like part of the family – they simply adored him. Each night after walking me home, he would come in for a cup of tea, charm the socks off my parents, and then, as I took him to the door, he'd kiss me softly on the lips and tell me I was the loveliest girl in the whole wide world.

One night, six months into our relationship, we were practising *Queen Of The Night* by Mozart for fun – seeing whether I could hit all the high notes. We'd gone through it three times without me getting there and then finally, on the fourth rendition, I did it – every note reached, pitch perfect. We were so excited that we spontaneously polkaed around the hall and then afterwards, he kissed me passionately on the lips and asked me to marry him and I said, 'Yes!' without a moment's hesitation. I knew without question that it could only be him. No one else had ever come this close to bringing me such unalloyed happiness, had made me feel so joyful to be alive. All previous sweethearts had simply paled into insignificance since I had met him.

I won't bore you with the details of the wedding, other than to say, it was a musical affair, the minister indulging us with four extra hymns, the choir singing in harmonies we had arranged ourselves. Nothing like a church full of people belting out a Charles Wesley accompanied by a thirty strong choir singing the harmonies. Even now, though my faith faded long ago, I still sometimes pop into the local Methodist church just for the pleasure of singing *Thine Be The Glory* and *Great Is Thy Faithfulness* at full blast.

I would love to tell you that my wedding day was the happiest day of my life, but that evening was when I first sensed that something wasn't right and it tarnished what had indeed, until then, been a wonderful occasion. I was a virgin so didn't know much about bedroom matters but I did know enough to know that as soon as we reached our hotel suite, the bridegroom should want to take his new bride straight to bed. But instead, Jack hesitated and asked if I would like a drink whilst pouring himself one twice the size of his usual tipple and gulping it down anxiously. At first, I thought, like me, he was nervous and just needed a little 'Dutch Courage' so I joined him in a sherry. But an hour passed and still nothing – he hadn't come near me. All he wanted to do was drink and talk about how the hymns had sounded, and I could feel my excited anticipation morphing into anxiety. Unsure of how to stop him from sinking into a drunken abyss, I decided to sing and instantly he lit up and joined in. By the time we got to *A Nightingale Sang In Berkley Square*, we were slow dancing, and finally the dancing turned to kissing and we moved to the bed. It wasn't that it didn't happen. It did, but it was fumbling and awkward. Jack kept his eyes tight shut throughout and went soft before technically he should have been done. I knew that something, fundamental had gone awry because none of the tiny few things my mother had told me to expect had happened. It hadn't even hurt that much. Afterwards, Jack rolled onto his back without looking at me and was deadly silent. Several minutes passed, and then finally, he squeezed my hand and said 'I love you.'

He then turned on his side, facing away from me. And that was that. I lay there, knowing that nothing was right but not having sufficient vocabulary in my head to explain it.

The rest of the honeymoon was much the same. Blissful days of laughing, walking and talking. Then at night, an awkward or embarrassing encounter, leaving me feeling inadequate and insecure. I started to wonder whether it was *me*. Maybe I wasn't sexy enough for him. I knew I was pretty but I'd never really been one for fashion. I dressed nicely in good quality clothes but didn't go in for make up or jewellery and I certainly had never thought it necessary to glam up for meeting Jack. Our affinity had been so powerful that I guess I assumed that he desired me the way I desired him, but suddenly I wondered whether he actually found me frumpy and plain. So when I returned to Swansea after ten days of honeymoon, I decided I needed to reassess my image. I didn't want to be too dramatic but I invested in two low cut blouses and two skirts with a split in the back, a nice pair of high heals and some bright red lipstick. I even bought myself some rollers to put a curl in my hair.

The first Saturday evening we were back, I made dinner and then before dishing it out, I popped upstairs and dressed up in my new attire, feeling excited and sexy – loving the idea of making my new husband finally ravish me. But when I came downstairs and entered our tiny dining room, all dolled up and raring to go, instead of jumping up from the table and sweeping me into a passionate embrace, Jack looked decidedly uncomfortable, finally getting up only to suggest he help serve dinner. Deflated and slightly mortified that he'd shown not even a flicker of desire, I followed him into the kitchen and together we dished out our food in silence and then made stunted conversation as we ate. Once we were done, he told me he had a headache and asked did I mind if he went out for a walk on his own to see if he could clear it. After he left the house, I ran upstairs and hurled myself on our bed weeping. I felt like he thought me quite ugly. I cleaned off my make-up, changed into my nightie and lay in the dark, deciding to pretend I was asleep when he came back so he couldn't witness my shame. He was away for almost two hours and on his return, he crept into our bed and put his arms around me, holding me like he had never held me before. And I wondered whether maybe I was just unlucky – that he did have a terrible headache after all, and perhaps if I tried again the next night, things would lead to more than just a fabulous cuddle.

But no. I dressed up again the following night, this time in the other new outfit I'd purchased, and the same thing happened again. He could barely look at me and rather than pin me to the rug, he went out for another long walk and came back and held me yet tighter.

After work on the Monday evening, we met at the church for the first time since coming home from our honeymoon. I was dressed in my usual teaching attire and as before, we played blissful music together until it was gone dark. Jack had started laughing again and we even did a little dance around the hall before we left. When we returned home, he led me upstairs and turned out the light and we made love in our clothes in the pitch black, and at last, it was successful from start to finish. I tried to work out what was different, and I realised that it was the first time we had played music together properly since we had married and thought maybe that was it. Maybe he needed to play music to want to make love – and it was nothing to do with how I dressed at all.

And for the next few nights, the same thing happened and I came to believe this was true. We played, we sang, we danced, we came home, we made love in the dark in our clothes. And I started to relax. But then on Saturday, he was fidgety all day, unable to settle, not really wanting to play music and looking out of the window, like an animal trapped at the zoo. After dinner, he said he needed his 'head clearing walk' and within moments, he was grabbing his coat and almost running down the road in the direction of the sea. When he returned, he did not attempt to make love to me but instead snuggled up and told me how much he loved me. Confused but relieved to hear the words, I let him stroke my hair and tell me how happy he was to have married me. Then on Sunday night, he did exactly the same again.

It must have been three or four months that things continued like this – week nights after playing music, him making love to me in the dark in my clothes, and then on Saturdays and Sundays, him going off and coming back late, then holding me and whispering sweet nothings in my ear.

I wasn't the kind of woman who discussed private things with family or friends and in spite of my confusion, I still felt close to Jack and knew he meant it when he told me he loved me. It was just that things were so bizarre when it came to making love. Then one Saturday afternoon, I was downstairs baking with Rachmaninov full blast on the gramophone, and couldn't find my hanky so went upstairs to look for it. I had just reached the threshold of our bedroom when I heard a strange shuffling sound and I stopped to look through the inch gap opening of the door. And there I saw my husband with his penis in his hand frantically masturbating whilst staring down into the garden below. At first, I froze – not knowing what to do – but then as he began to reach a crescendo, I slipped downstairs not wanting him to know I had seen him. I rushed into the garden to see who this woman was who had made my husband so aroused that he had stood there in the middle of our bedroom unable to contain himself. But to my horror, I discovered our next door neighbour Mr Llewellyn, chopping wood, shirtless in the early spring sun. And suddenly, I realised my husband didn't want to be a husband at all. He wanted something altogether different indeed.

By now you must think I was so stupid. How could I possibly not have known I had married a gay man? Why hadn't I spotted the signs? But you have to remember things were different back then. We knew that men going with men was a sin and against the law, and boys showing any hint of effeminacy were called 'nancies' until they stopped doing whatever it was that was considered wrong. But the concept of gay people – gay men – wasn't really even thought about or discussed. When Jack had courted me and done nothing but kiss me softly on the lips goodbye, I'd assumed it was because he was a gentleman. How could I have possibly known any different? So as I stood in our garden, trying to absorb the fact that my husband desired the man next door more than he desired me, I didn't have a proper name for it. I was simply horrified and broken hearted.

Of course, like any woman from my background, I said absolutely nothing, but instead, tried to work out what it all meant. I looked back on the past four months and saw a pattern – if he was high from music and it was dark and I was not naked, he wanted me enough to make love to me. If there was no music and I dressed femininely to make him want me, the exact opposite occurred. Therefore, I had to find a way to give him what he actually needed. And so I did an experiment. The next morning, I told him I was going to do some gardening and asked if I could borrow a pair of his trousers and a shirt as I didn't have any of my own. He did not question it and we were about the same size so I put on the outfit he provided and a pair of his old shoes, tied my hair back tightly, and then spent an hour in the garden while he played piano indoors. When I came in, still dressed in his attire, I joined him at the piano and picked up my violin. Together we played the *Kreutzer Sonata* by Beethoven and on the final note, he looked up and down at me for the first time with a flash of lust, so I grabbed his hand and led him upstairs, where we made love in the light and finally both enjoyed it.

And so, at the first opportunity, I went out and bought myself a selection of men's clothes to wear in the privacy of our own home and a selection of women's clothes that were slightly more masculine to wear in the outside world. And I can honestly say that for the next few months, Jack and I made love and enjoyed it every night – still in the dark during the week when I looked like a woman, but in the light at weekends when I looked like a man. It had worked. No more long walks because of headaches, no more trouble at the beginning or halfway through. When he didn't see me as a woman, my husband desired me.

I didn't mind. I didn't. I know that sounds crazy. But I was madly in love with him and he was so lovely in every other way. Kind and considerate. Always helping with the household tasks – never expecting me to do everything just because I was a woman. And the music. Oh the endless music. Our little world was so happy. It was a small sacrifice to look like a man for him, in order for us to get what we both needed. Our life together finally worked. Until, of course, I fell pregnant…

Within a few months of being expectant, my belly swelling and my breasts growing larger, I was back to wearing flowing dresses all of the time. Anything else was impossible. Jack was as lovely as ever, taking over more of the housework, indulging my food cravings and rubbing my feet. He was excited about the baby and would lie with his head on my stomach singing lullabies to our unborn child. But it wasn't long before I'd catch him looking out of the window with a pained expression on his face, not knowing I was watching him. We were no longer making love, and I knew that it wasn't just because I was four months pregnant, but because I looked like a woman again and he didn't desire me when I looked female.

After a while, the long walks at night to clear his head recommenced. The first week, it was just the once and he came back looking peaceful, and the next day he spent hours composing, playing and singing. He seemed content again… for a few days… but soon the restless sadness returned, and before long, he went out for another walk – only for the same thing to occur the following day – renewed musical bliss, laughter and creativity. Within three weeks, Jack was going out nearly every night. I think deep down I knew what it might be. Even when you don't know about these things, you sort of do. But I guess I had to see for myself. To really understand what it was, who *he* was.

So one night, now nearly six months pregnant, I followed him, slipping out just after he left in the direction of the docks. It didn't take long to catch up enough to see exactly where he was. He walked down to a spot not far from where one of the merchant navy ships was docked. And after a few minutes, an enormous man dressed in sailing garb approached him and together they walked to an area of bombed out factories and scrub land. I followed them stealthily, but close enough to see. Creeping as near as I could in the dim light. I must admit I was still shocked at what I witnessed. My husband was bent over with his trousers around his ankles letting himself be pummelled, yes literally pummelled, by a man nearly twice his size and almost screaming with pleasure – his face wild with ecstatic joy. As I watched, in stunned silence, I realised that even my attempts to dress like a man had given him nothing but a poor substitute for what he actually wanted. The thing that he needed most in the world, I simply could not give. And I vowed then that I would never again fool myself into believing that he actually wanted me. This is who he was. And his need to be taken by a man was, in fact, even greater than my own.

[SARA PAUSES]

I know what you're asking now. Why didn't I confront him? Why didn't I leave? But you forget, this was the late 1950s. I didn't even know the proper term for what I had witnessed. All I knew is that religion and society looked on it as a sin worthy of burning in hell and the law forbade it. How could I possibly even begin a conversation with him? And women did not leave their husbands back then. Not if they wanted to remain in their community. It simply wasn't done. And for a pregnant woman to leave… Well that would have been the end of everything. Family, friends, church, community. Everything. So I said nothing.

Instead, I decided to settle for what I had and make the most of it. When he came back brimming with energy, I would encourage him to compose straight away rather than waiting, and then the following morning, we would play it together. And if it was a song, I would help write the lyrics. We would become lost in musical bliss and laugh and chatter and dance and cuddle. He was happier and more creative than I'd ever known him. And when our child arrived – a girl we named Bronwyn – he held her in his arms and promised her he would be the best daddy in the world, and I cried with happiness.

Unlike the husbands of my friends and peers, Jack helped me with every aspect of being a mother – from getting up at three o'clock in the morning to rock our baby back to sleep, to changing and washing dirty nappies. Our life was so deeply loving that him not wanting to make love to me, felt like a tiny trade off for such satisfaction and contentment in every other area of my life. So what if he went down the docks every night to get pummelled by a random sailor? He was happy. I was happy. Our baby was happy.

Don't judge me. I am not a victim. Hear the rest of my story first. But before I tell you any more, do ask yourself this: Do you know anyone, anyone at all who has found absolutely everything they ever wanted or needed in their marriage? In my experience, all women give up a huge part of themselves, sometimes the most vibrant, creative part of their being, to make their marriage work. I actually – even now – after everything that happened subsequently – still think I got off lightly in my forfeit compared to some of my friends.

Anyway, after a couple of years of this new realigned happiness, I realised that if I wanted to have another child, I had to make Jack remember he needed to make love to me as well as cuddle. It may sound silly to you, but we would curl up in bed every night and then simply fall asleep. I never tried to touch him and he never tried to touch me. At this point he did not know I knew about his sexual needs but I think he knew I no longer expected him to perform husbandly duties. So I had to make a decision – should I tell him I knew he desired men not women but I wanted another baby – or should I just do what was required to make him want me enough so I would end up pregnant anyway? I realised that I did not wish to shatter our happy home with agonising conversations so instead, I started wearing trousers and shirts in the house again at weekends, tied my hair back and this time, even added the tiniest spot of his aftershave at my neck. And then after a few weekends, one Saturday when he returned home late, I asked him to sing with me at the piano instead of compose, and once we had been united by our mutual love of music, I led him upstairs to bed.

It worked again. Men are much easier to manipulate than you think. Even gay ones. After eight weekends of dressing like a man, I was pregnant. And like last time, as soon as I began to dress and look like a woman again, our love making stopped. At least this time I was prepared for it. I had got what I wanted, another baby growing inside my womb. And the music played on.

Stupidly, I believed that things would be pretty and jolly forever. And they were for a few more months. Until it happened. The event that changed everything. The event that destroyed all parts of my existence, the bomb that dropped in the centre of my life – our life.

One night, when I was now seven months pregnant with our second child, Jack did not return home at the usual time but instead, at just gone midnight, there was an urgent rat-a-tat-tat on the door and I opened it to find Dylan – our local beat bobby – standing there looking white and gulping. My first reaction was to scream – believing Jack was dead. Maybe he had been run over or had tripped in the rubble by the docks and smashed his head? But no. It wasn't that. It was, in many ways, a more terrible event for both of us. 'I'm sorry Mrs Lewis, I… I…' Constable Dylan hesitated. 'I…. I… I've come to inform you that your husband has been arrested for… Gross Indecency with another man…'

You have to remember times were very different back then. And no one could survive a scandal like that in a town like Swansea. We are not talking about a densely populated city like London where people could move three miles away to the other side and start again without a soul knowing who they were. This was a metaphorical death. On being convicted and sent down, Jack's life in Swansea was over for good. But what you probably don't understand – and why I chose to stay with him and indeed move to London – so was mine. Think for a minute. A society where homosexuality was universally condemned as a sin and a crime. A town where everyone knew everyone else. What was I to become? The object of gossip? Pity? Scandal? Could I really have ever had a normal life again – even if I got divorced? No.

My devastated parents, brothers and sisters wanted me to divorce and disown him. They thought this was the only way to salvage our reputation as a family. But they were only thinking of themselves. Not me. My life would forever be tarnished by the scandal – 'Ooh, look, there goes Mrs Lewis. Did you know her ex-husband was sent to jail for being buggered by a sailor down the docks? Sorry for her, I am.'

[SARA PAUSES, LOOKING SAD]

Jack pleaded guilty so there was no trial – only a sentencing, which I did not attend because I knew it would kill him to have me there. Eighteen months he was given. During the following four weeks, now almost nine months pregnant, I left the house just once to finally visit him in prison. My youngest brother, Michael, the only one of us who had a car, drove me to Cardiff where Jack was being held and waited outside while I went in.

When Jack saw me, he crumbled. Me, just days away from giving birth to his second child, and him, in abject shame, his life in tatters. He could barely speak through the tears. I held both his hands in mine and told him that I loved him and that nothing he had done could change that. He looked at me seriously then and asked, 'Even now you know what I am?' At which point, I shook my head and cupped his cheek in my hand. 'My darling boy, I've known exactly what you are for most of our marriage and I have still loved you just as much as I always did.'
He started to howl then – so loudly that I had to calm him down – as everyone around us began staring and the guards looked set to move in to break up our visit.
'Listen,' I said. 'I have been in touch with your sister in London. She says she can sort us out a flat not far from her house in Clapham. As soon as the baby is born, I will go there and then, when you are out, if you want to, we can start again.' Jack looked surprised at this and said, 'You mean it will be like it was before? We can pretend this never happened?'
I shook my head and was firm with him then. 'No. Not like before. If we do this we have to be honest. No more pretences. We have to face up to who you are and what

that means for both of us… but I have to ask you something first…'
'What?'
'Do you want to have a relationship with a man like the one you had with me, or is what you got caught for doing just a thing that you need to feel satisfied?'
He gulped and trembled, then grasped both of my hands again and said, 'You are the love of my life. I will never love anyone else the way I love you. I want to be with you always and I want to be a father to our children.'
I stared at him for a while trying to be sure he meant it before finally responding. 'Then come to London,' I said. 'And we will work out the rest once you're there.'

[SARA PAUSES AGAIN, LOOKING PAINED]

I didn't visit Jack in prison again. Four days later, I gave birth to our second daughter, Glynnis. Then shortly after that, when I was well enough to travel, Michael drove me to London and I moved into the flat that Jack's sister had arranged. None of my family wanted me to leave but I think they knew after countless arguments, discussions and debates, that even if I didn't take Jack back, in the end I would be better off in London. My mother wept as I left and I promised her I would come back as often as I could so she could see the girls. My father took me to one side and said, 'I am sorry this happened to you, Sara. But you do know that if you take him back, he can never set foot in this house again, don't you?' I nodded, kissed him on the cheek and then got in the car without looking back. My life in Swansea was over.

Once I had settled in London, I had a choice to make. Was I going to relegate myself to a life without intimacy or could I, like Jack, find satisfaction elsewhere? I knew I could not, and indeed would not, know how to have anonymous encounters. Such opportunities did not exist for women back then in the way they do now. But I wondered whether perhaps I might meet a man like me who needed an 'arrangement' rather than a relationship. But again, a woman making those kind of arrangements was unheard of. Women had very limited autonomy over such matters. As it was, I fell into a relationship with a man called Simon who lived in the same building. He was single, having broken up from his fiancé just before their wedding, and had moved away by taking a job as an engineer on the London Underground.

One day we got chatting in the hallway, and he helped me upstairs with my shopping. He asked me where my husband was and I said, 'In prison for fraud.' This is what Jack and I had agreed would be our story. People forgave fraud. They did not forgive sodomy. As he put the shopping down on the counter and turned to me, I saw a dart of attraction in his eyes and I realised that this might be my opportunity to have a sex life of my own. Simon was a good looking man. Very good looking, in fact. And extremely masculine. And so, gradually, I let him help me with jobs around the flat and when he was due, I found myself putting on lipstick and adding little extra touches of femininity to my attire – even buying myself a shorter skirt than I would have ever considered before. The more femininely I dressed, the more he looked at me, and the longer he stayed around. Then, one evening a few weeks in, he knocked on the door late at night after the children were asleep. Smelling of beer and unsteady on his feet, he asked me, 'Do you ever get lonely without your husband here?' And I, knowing it was now or never, said 'yes' and stepped forward.

I have to admit, I really enjoyed the first few months of that relationship. I enjoyed being wanted for being female. Being taken by a man that actually desired women, gruff and selfish though he was. He never had any trouble or hesitation. He liked doing it to me and I liked having it done. If I wore a low cut blouse, short skirt and put on bright red lipstick, we would end up in bed almost immediately, barely saying hello. I even bought frilly knickers – knowing intuitively, that wearing them would make him want me even more. I felt female. All woman. At last. But then, a funny thing happened…

I started to get bored. Yes, Simon liked having me, and yes, sometimes I had an orgasm. But he was no more interested in *my* pleasure than Jack had been – he was only interested in his own. And what's more, he wasn't actually that interested in *me*. Other than the standard, 'How are you, love?' he never asked anything about me or my interests, just talked about himself. And… well – I think ultimately this is what killed it for me in the end – it turned out that he didn't know anything about music other than the pop songs he listened to on the wireless. He had never been to concert, never sung in a choir, didn't know Bach from Brahms. Nothing. There was no way this man was ever going to dance around the living room with me to celebrate that I'd hit all the high notes in *Queen Of The Night*.

So gradually, as the novelty wore off, I stopped dressing up for him and began talking about Jack coming home soon, until eventually, one night there was no knock on my door, nor any night after that. Two weeks later, Simon moved out of his flat and I never saw him again. In all honesty, I was relieved. I'd got what I wanted and needed, and now I could get on with my life without insecurity. But it was after this, that I promised myself I would never, ever dress for a man again. I would only ever dress for *me*. Wear what *I* wanted to wear. Look how *I* wanted to look.

When Jack finally joined me in London, he was a broken man. Prison is not an easy ordeal for anyone but for a 'nancy boy', it is as tough as you can get. Bullied, battered and occasionally raped, his soul had been crushed by the regime. My visit was the only one he'd had – his family, apart from Gwenno his sister, who had found us the flat, had disowned him. He had been totally alone. I honestly think if it hadn't been for meeting his new daughter, he might never have recovered. As it was, in those first few months, I tended to him like another child – feeding him soft and comforting foods, holding him in my arms and rocking him while he cried, and soothing him after nightmares.

Then, when he was strong again, we sat down and talked. I had used up all our savings and had been living off the charity of my parents and his sister, and things needed to change before resentments crept in. With a criminal record, Jack could never teach in a school or be a church organist again but he could teach private music lessons to adults. So we decided that I would go back to work as a full-time teacher, and he would look after the girls in the day and give music lessons in the evenings and on weekends. That part of the arrangement was the easy bit to discuss but I knew, now he was recovered, I had to tackle the hard part too. So one evening when I saw the faraway look in his eye, the one that had landed him in prison in the first place, I sat him down and said, 'Jack. I can never change who you are and I don't want to anymore. But I cannot let you risk this life or that of the girls by saying it's ok for you to go out and meet men in dark places. I have lost one life for you already and I cannot lose another.'

He stopped me then and vowed he would never go with a man again, at which point, for the first time ever, I was angry with him. 'Don't you dare make promises you can't keep! We both know that's not true and I won't be lied to. I saw you, Jack. I followed you one night. I know exactly what you want and how you like it, and I know full well that a time will come when you won't be able to help yourself. So shut up, show me some respect and listen.'

He was red then – shamed and mortified that I had seen him with a sailor – unable to look me in the eye. So I stopped shouting and spoke firmly instead. 'The only thing I ask is this: if you want to do that, then you must do it in a safe place. I will be taking the girls home once a month to see their grandparents. While I am gone, you can do whatever you want with who ever you want in this flat. But if I find out that you have been at it in toilets, bushes or bombed out buildings, then I am leaving you for good. Is that clear?'
He nodded, still looking deeply ashamed.
'Do we have a deal?' I pressed.
He nodded again.

And so the next phase of our marriage began. And I have to tell you, those next twenty-four years were the happiest years of my life. Our home was filled with music once more. Our children learned piano, violin and clarinet and oh, how we sang. We were proud parents watching our girls grow into fine young women. Bronwyn went on to be a concert pianist and Glynnis became a primary school teacher, like me.

Jack kept to his promise. He never again went out at night. But as agreed, once a month I visited my family in Swansea and he had the flat to himself. We didn't talk about it but I knew he used it for the intended purpose. I could tell by the way he was when I returned. We slept in the same bed at night but we never made love again, only cuddled and kissed goodnight before turning to sleep. And to be honest, I didn't mind. Somewhere along the way, my sexual desire for him had died and my feelings of 'in love' had morphed into 'family love' and I was happy. I didn't even take a lover – I didn't want anything to shatter our precious little world full of music, comfort and care. But of course, life is never kind forever and truly happy endings exist for no one. And eventually, our idyllic little life was smashed into a thousand pieces for a second time.

[SARA PAUSES AND A TEAR IS SHED AND WIPED AWAY]

Sorry… it's just that this next part is hard for me. In late 1983, a few weeks after having what he thought was a bad dose of flu, Jack developed a dark patch on his right shin and went to the doctors, only to have it confirmed a week later, what we already both knew in our hearts – that he had contracted AIDS.

As a straight woman, with a gay husband, I never thought for a moment allowing Jack to use our marital bed to fulfil needs that I could not, would ultimately lead to the encounter that killed him. When I look back now, as a 'receiver' rather than a 'giver', Jack never stood a chance of dodging that disease. Perhaps, if it had been the other way around he might, just might, have escaped it… but he was unlucky. They were all unlucky, those men…

Straight people can be very judgemental about that generation of gay men – saying that they brought their early deaths upon themselves, and if they hadn't slept around then it wouldn't have spread like the plague. But they forget that gay men had already broken the taboo concerning sleeping with people outside of marriage – and could have sex without fear of pregnancy – so why would they have considered that having sex with lots of men, rather than just one man, was even an issue?

The children knew nothing about Jack's sexuality, or so we thought. Therefore, when the crushing diagnosis was upon us, we told them it must have been from a dirty needle when he'd donated blood. It wasn't until years later that Bronwyn told me that she and Glynnis had known since they were teenagers about Jack's stay in prison. One of their cousins had told them during an argument and they'd asked my sister if it was true. So as it turned out, like us, our daughters had not wanted to break the magic of our happy family and had played along with our explanation, knowing it wasn't the case.

The last two months of Jack's life were spent on an AIDS ward in a hospital in North London. I cannot describe the pain for me, Bronwyn and Glynnis of watching him wither away before us. Each day a little thinner, a little weaker, the light slowly fading from his cobalt blue eyes. At first we would all sing together as a family – vowing to make music together right until the end. But when it came to his final days, Jack no longer had the strength to join us and we had to sing for him. The night before he died, he started drifting in and out of consciousness. After the girls went home, I stayed with him and stroked his soft thatch of greying hair, singing to him gently. Just before he fell asleep for good, he reached for me and rasped, 'You are the love of my life. I'm sorry I caused you so much pain.' And I, knowing that this was goodbye, kissed him gently on the lips and replied, 'And you are the love of my life and a little pain was more than worth it for all the joy and music you gave me.' At which point his eyes closed and I held his hand until he was gone. And that night, part of me died with him.

[SARA PAUSES FOR SEVERAL MOMENTS, STANDS UP AND LOOKS ACROSS THE CITYSCAPE TO COMPOSE HERSELF, THEN RETURNS TO HER SEAT.]

So what about me? Widowed before reaching fifty, did I find love again? Well, kind of. I know you would love me to tell you that I met a new man with a personality like Jack's but with the heterosexual drive of Simon. But that's a fairytale – you do know that, don't you? One in a million women meet a man like that… and I simply did not.

However, I did eventually fall a little bit in love again. No one tells you when you're young that there are different strengths of 'in love', but I assure you there are. The miles between 'madly in love' and a 'little bit in love' though are substantial. But with the children both married and loneliness stripping away what little sense of purpose I had left, when love came again, I embraced it welcomingly.

Five years after Jack passed away, Richard started teaching science at the same school as me and with him being recently widowed too, we had a fundamental understanding of one another. Richard didn't play a musical instrument or sing – he didn't even know how to dance – but he did like listening to classical music and accompanying me to concerts. He was also a full-blooded heterosexual. I kept to my promise to myself that I would never dress to please a man again but he liked my style and he never needed coaxing when it came to making love.

Richard and I were together for thirty years until he passed away – exactly the same amount of time I was with Jack. We had a good marriage. A safe marriage. And I did care for him. But did he worship me the way Jack did? No. Was our house filled with music and laughter from morning until night? No. Did my heart somersault every time he smiled at me? No. You are lucky, deeply lucky, if you get that twice in one lifetime.

And this is why I am sitting here telling you all this – why I have told you my story. Because I want you to know that *all* love is precious. And *all* love is worth it… But the most important thing… the bit that I really want you to remember is…

[SARA TAKES A DEEP BREATH]

Sometimes the love of your life is not your lover. They are your best friend.

Monologue 3.

People Like Us

[LUCINDA, AGED EIGHTY-FOUR, IS WEARING EXPENSIVE BEIGE CASHMERE TROUSERS AND CREAM SILK BLOUSE. SHE IS SITTING DRINKING TEA IN A LARGE CONSERVATORY. SHE SPEAKS WITH AN UPPER CLASS ENGLISH ACCENT.]

Contrary to popular opinion, it is possible to make an absolute hash of one's love life even in one's eighties. Particularly if one has hesitated. No, I must be completely honest now. If one has *resisted* because the person one has unexpectedly fallen in love with is of the same sex.

[LUCINDA PAUSES]

Do not misunderstand me. This is not the first time I have fallen in love with another woman. I have had relationships with women, as well as men, since I was eleven years old. It has been the coming out part that I have struggled with.

It is, in fact, my personal belief that no woman is one hundred percent heterosexual. I know some of you may think this a somewhat contentious assertion but if you are listening to my story and claim to be a heterosexual woman, then I request you pause for a moment and consider. Was there a girl at school on whom you had a crush? Or perhaps a female teacher? Has there been a female singer or film idol who was the 'exception to the rule' – a woman so utterly entrancing that you wanted to kiss her and touch her, in spite of not wanting to kiss or touch the pretty girl standing next to you? In my day, the 'exception to the rule' was usually Katharine Hepburn, Greta Garbo or Marlene Dietrich. But I suspect that these days, the women who would make a straight girl turn, are completely different and not within my sphere of knowledge. This is what I mean when I posit that no woman is one hundred percent straight. Nor indeed, one hundred percent gay, for that matter. I've yet to meet a woman who calls herself a lesbian who hasn't had a passing fancy of a man – even the most dyed in the wool lesbians I have encountered have been attracted to at least one male film star.

However, I am not a woman who has passing crushes on other women. I am genuinely attracted to and fall in love with women as well as men. But until today, I have never openly admitted it. For women from my background, being bisexual meant that you presented to the world as straight. Having an out in the open relationship with someone of the same sex was, and still to a certain degree is, forbidden. 'People Like Us' simply do not come out.

Let me expand a little. I went to the kind of girls' public boarding school which was so elite that we referred to the groundskeepers and kitchen staff as 'the proles'. We were educated well, with the expectation of doing absolutely nothing with that education other than becoming a most excellent wife of an elite public boarding school boy who would eventually become a politician, a judge, a brigadier general or a surgeon.

I need to explain to you about elite girls' boarding schools, lesbianism and bisexuality. But before I elaborate further, ask yourself this… Have you ever met a woman from *my* background who is fully out of the closet? I'm not talking rich women on the cusp of middle and upper class here. I'm talking of the establishment. Do you know any woman, even a younger woman in these enlightened times, who is 'out and proud'? A woman who goes on marches and takes her lover home to meet her parents? I'd be very surprised if you did.

Yes, I know, I know, you are thinking about famous gay aristocrats, aren't you? But male and gay is different from female and gay. And besides, only the ones who are absolute artistic geniuses are made exceptions for. Even Vita Sackville West, by remaining in Great Britain, had to conform to the institution of marriage – all her affairs with women were seen as scandalous and shameful, and rumours had to be quashed. The generation before me who lived through 'The Roaring Twenties' did have a now somewhat romanticised clutch of lesbians who escaped to Paris, endeavouring to lead authentic lives while trying desperately not to get cut off from their family incomes. But not all of them managed it. Some were disowned altogether, others eventually returned home and married men as instructed. Besides, by the time my generation came along, World War II had put paid to any freedoms those women had gained. My generation conformed to heterosexual marriage as women from the past had indeed conformed.

My apologies, I digress again. I was talking about my school where I was trained not to come out of the closet under any circumstances. My school, like most other girls' boarding schools was, in actual fact, a hotbed of lesbian desire. Consider again for a moment my assertion that no woman is one hundred percent heterosexual. All those girls cooped up together day and night with an all female teaching staff. Did you really think we never touched one another?

Of course, there were degrees of interaction. From those who had intense silent crushes, to those who fiddled and fumbled a little in the dorms but never quite went all the way. And then there were girls like me, who were rolling around in the hay from the age of eleven. The stables were where girls such as I found one another and explored one another. And the teachers, many of whom themselves had done plenty of rolling in the hay back in their day, never, ever came into the stables after six o'clock in the evening. It was an unwritten rule.

Let me talk briefly about the teachers. I told you earlier that we, women of my class, were not permitted to come out. However, there were places where, so long as one said absolutely nothing and kept it absolutely private, lesbian sexuality was and still is tolerated.

If one were so lesbian one simply could not find a way of becoming a good wife, submitting oneself to a man, or having intercourse with a man, then there were only two options for an adult female. If one were exceptionally academic, one could become a don at an elite university. Alternatively, if one were reasonably academic, one could become a teacher in an elite public boarding school. One would no longer be invited to social events, other than christenings, weddings and funerals, but one's reputation was sufficiently intact for one not to be a source of scandal. Out of sight. Out of mind.

Sadly, though, if one were not bright enough to escape into academia of any kind, then one simply had no choice but to marry someone one did not love.

[LUCINDA PAUSES BRIEFLY]

Or become an outcast…

By outcast, I mean *outcast* – cast out. No inheritance. Disowned. Totally alone. We have our own world you know. We live in a parallel universe only inhabited by People Like Us. Behind black doors in Soho and Mayfair are private members clubs to which only *we* are permitted. *Our* golf courses are not your golf courses. *Our* five star hotels are not your five star hotels. Even if you are 'new money' and buy one of our deserted mansions, you will never be One Of Us. Never be a part of *our* set.

If you are not from our background, but went to a good university, you might briefly have thought we were the same as you – just richer. The chances are we came to the students' union now and then, we may have been your good friend or perhaps even slept with you in a moment of arch rebellion. But were you ever invited to one of our places or events, or did we only come to yours? When we brought Mummy into university for a visit, did we for some strange reason only introduce Mummy to those who went to boarding school too and accidently forget about you? And within two years of graduation, were we still going out drinking with you on a Friday night? Did you ever, in fact, see us again?

I have gone off at another tangent, I know. But only so you fully comprehend why I ended up making the choices I made and causing myself untold misery as a consequence...

I'd surmise that by this point in my account, some of you are sitting there, already hating me with a passion, thinking, 'Why should I be listening to the rambling regrets of a posh old bitch, who has had all of life's privileges and none of its hardships?' And I would agree. But I am not telling you my story so you feel sorry for me. I just want you to hear how someone in her eighties could make a complete dog's dinner of her love life.

So, as I began to recount, I spent a lot of time in the stables in my youth. I played around with and eventually made love with dozens of girls. In the sixth form, I even had a more formal relationship with a girl named Abigail. But I never expected this relationship to last and neither did she. Even though we absolutely adored one another, and had the most intimate union imaginable, we spent much of our time chatting about whom we might marry and whether we wanted to go to finishing school or, in my case, university, first. There was no scenario where we thought we would actually be together. We simply assumed that if the feelings were still there, and circumstances allowed, we would carry on seeing each other in secret.

We both liked boys as well as girls, so the option of remaining on the periphery of the set and becoming a don or a teacher, did not appeal to us. And besides, I wanted to become a doctor – which was controversial enough.

When I told my parents that I wanted to go into medicine, they were not altogether surprised. Nonetheless, in 1953, it was still almost unheard of for a woman from my set to take up such a profession. Do not confuse me with the private school girls a rung or two down the ladder. I mean from my background. Old Money. The Aristocracy. The Elite. Families who are Royalty or marry into Royalty. Women Like Us did not have careers.

I remember my mother sobbing, terrified that my wish to become a doctor would bring shame and scandal upon the family. But my father, who was a prominent MP, looked at me seriously and said, 'Lucinda, if this were your sister asking, I would refuse my consent. However, you have the most exceptional mind I have ever encountered in a female and for this reason I will allow it. But on one condition… If you pursue this controversial route, you must promise me that you will become no less than a surgeon, with a Harley Street practice and be an expert in your field.'

And so I did.

I did exactly that. I went to university, studied medicine and then specialised in endocrine surgery. One might even say I was trained for a career in slitting other ladies' throats!

[LUCINDA CHUCKLES - IT'S CLEARY A JOKE SHE'S USED BEFORE. THEN, SLIGHTLY

EMBARRASSED, COUGHS A LITTLE BEFORE CARRYING ON.]

Anyway, as expected, Abigail and I drifted once I went to university and she went to finishing school. By the time she married Rafe, aged nineteen, I was already courting a fellow student named Jeremy with whom I technically lost my virginity, despite having made love with over a dozen girls in every imaginable way before then. From then on, I made it my priority to sleep only with men. After all, I needed to find a suitable husband and continuing on sleeping with girls would inevitably lead to dead end relationships and pain.

I am not going to sit here and tell you I did not enjoy making love with men. I am not a lesbian. Making love with a man feels completely different and services an entirely different set of physical and emotional needs and desires, from making love with a woman. I have always wanted both but have been forced since adulthood to choose the one of which society approves.

There are those who claim that desiring both sexes is greedy. I disagree. It's not greed, it's need. I am a complex woman with a great many needs. No one person, male or female could hope to fulfil all of them. I don't know why people think there is anything unusual about that.

Marriage of course, is an entirely different entity and involves a commitment to one person irrespective of other desires. During the third year of my degree, I met Sebastian, who was two years my senior, and the man who would become my husband for forty years. I was very much in love with Sebastian. Intelligent, tall, dark and handsome, he had just qualified at the bar and was of course 'One Of Us'. He'd attended the correct school and came from a family whose name and land dated back to the eleventh century. There were no serious family chats to ascertain whether this was a suitable alliance. His credentials alone were enough for him to be regarded as the perfect match. My parents did not even ask me whether I loved him.

As it was, for the first twenty-five of our forty years together, Sebastian and I were happy. It wasn't until he reached his late forties and started sleeping with younger women that I finally fell out of love with him. He had, I think, until then remained faithful, but as with all marriages our love-making had become sporadic between having our children and maintaining high profile careers. And as his hair receded and lines became etched around his eyes, soon I was smelling other women's perfume on his clothes.

I won't lie and say it didn't hurt. It did... but I felt that we could continue on being married but both have lovers and remain friends. So once I had reconciled myself with the idea that he was never going to be true to me again, I decided to give into one of the many crushes I had fought off – the one I had on my secretary, Leona, who had been working for me for over five years, and had provided many a wild fantasy during my lonelier nights.

It was when Sebastian caught me in bed with Leona that I stopped loving him altogether. He was furious in a way that I had never witnessed before and told me my actions were reprehensible. I retorted that he was on at least his fourth secretary by now so why was it such a problem for me to be on my first? To which he replied that it was different for men. He could survive and our family would survive if he were caught sleeping with his secretary. Indeed it was almost expected that a man of his age and stature would have at least one mistress by now. But I could not. Not with a man and certainly not with a woman. I would tarnish our family name and ruin the marital prospects of our two daughters and the career prospects of our two sons.

It was his hypocrisy that made me lose what love for him I had remaining. But then with People Like Us, hypocrisy is rife. I mean, I have witnessed a woman who I went down on multiple times in the stables at school, stand next to her politician husband and nod emphatically while he condemned homosexuality as a transgression worthy of roasting in Hell. I have witnessed men who went to elite boarding schools, some of whom without doubt had relations with one another in the same way the girls did at mine, vote in Parliament against legislation to lower the age of consent, setting the fight for equality back by years as a consequence.

Never doubt the old adage. There really is one rule for us, and an entirely different rule for you.

This does not mean we should all be hated. There are plenty of us who are perfectly decent human beings who have tried to do some genuine good in this world. Flawed though I am, by becoming an endocrine surgeon, I both improved and saved countless lives – especially women's lives, as they are more prone to conditions such as thyrotoxicosis and hyperparathyroidism. Controversial though it was, I was allowed to continue operating even after I became a mother because I was so utterly brilliant in my field. There is a lot about me to detest, but not that. Becoming a surgeon is the only thing in my life I am truly proud of.

Anyway, after Sebastian caught me and made it clear in no uncertain terms that he would continue on sleeping with his secretary, but I had to stop sleeping with mine, our marriage became a frosty sea of toleration and keeping up appearances. We never made love again nor even pretended to have any affection left for one another.

[LUCINDA PAUSES]

Sebastian died aged sixty-three of a massive stroke. I did shed a tear at his passing. After all, he was the father of my children and grandfather to a growing brood of grandchildren. So in spite of the acrimony in the latter part of our marriage, I was nonetheless bereft and saddened.

[SHE PAUSES AGAIN]

A while after Sebastian died, I began sleeping with other people again – predominantly women whom I'd had encounters with at school and who had remained within my sphere. But whether they were widowed like me or being unfaithful, there was never any suggestion that such affairs would become full blown relationships. The rules were still the same as they had been over forty years previously.

Eventually though, once a fitting amount of time had passed, I found myself a male lover called Alexander who came from my set and could therefore escort me to social engagements. We were together for two years, but although we were terribly fond of one another, we were never really in love and inevitably he met someone else for whom he had those feelings, so we parted company amicably.

Then, as I grew older, romantic interactions with both sexes gradually diminished. And by the time I met Camilla, at the age of eighty, I had not made love with anyone for over three years.

I first encountered Camilla when I was invited to be the keynote speaker at a four day conference on Endocrine

Medicine, where I would talk about the pioneering work I had done in parathyroid surgery. Even though I had stopped practising at seventy-five, I still worked as a consultant and was a much esteemed figure in my field. Camilla, also an endocrine surgeon, based in Manchester, had organised the event. She was twenty years my junior, but I felt connected to her from the moment we first met. I'm not given to flights of fancy concerning spiritual matters, but there was something about this woman – the way in which we communicated, the things we discovered we had in common, my immediate attraction to her – it was as though we were fated to meet…

On the first evening of the conference, after delivering my lecture, I found myself spontaneously drawing her into me for a hug. What I wasn't prepared for though, was what this hug did to me. What *she* did to me. For suddenly I was engulfed by a wave of healing energy, so overwhelming in its potency, that it made me physically jolt, and I pulled away, unable to look her in the eye.

Many years ago, I had attended an event where the concept of the medical practitioner's 'healing touch' had been explored. And the speaker, a doctor who had been somewhat seduced by alternative medicine, had us experiment with laying hands on one another. Some of the participants said that they'd experienced a rush of healing energy surge through them, but I had felt nothing and had gone away thinking it a load of poppycock and New Age bunkum.

But this woman – this doctor – what her hug did to me – kept me awake all night. I simply could not stop thinking about her. Could not stop wanting her arms around me once again, and this time not to back away but instead, fall into her embrace.

Everything about her was wrong, of course. She was middle class so not of my background, far too young, and yet more alarmingly, totally open about being a lesbian. She looked like a lesbian, walked like a lesbian and talked like a lesbian. No one would ever have mistaken her for a heterosexual woman. She was a living advertisement for all things Sapphic. But nonetheless, in spite of her being utterly incorrect in every conceivable way, I knew that this was not going to be a passing crush and I had, in actual fact, fallen in love. Not love at first sight but love at first hug.

I categorically did not want to be in love with Camilla. Perhaps if she had been only a few years younger than I, or had had the same upbringing as I, then she would have understood why I could never have a relationship with a woman which was not clandestine by nature. But she was from the generation who had marched and fought for their right to love openly, without shame. A generation and a class who had simply refused to live in the shadows and keep their sexuality a secret. She was jeopardous, perhaps even disastrous to consider becoming involved with.

Over the next two days of the conference, I attempted to avoid her. Yet my efforts were in vain – for every time I even glanced in her direction, it was as though she somehow felt it and looked back at me immediately and smiled. However, whenever she approached me to actually converse, I remained distant and a little rude, unable to engage with her lest I gave my feelings away. I passed on all social activities and ordered room service in the evenings so I could avoid becoming further entangled. The power of the connection frightened me too greatly.

On the fourth day, I was due to deliver the concluding lecture and just before I left the wings to approach the podium, Camilla squeezed my hand, and the same tingling energy imbued with healing love rushed right through me. Turning to her in shock, I saw for the first time that she was in love with me too, even though she had not flirted, or gazed at me longingly, or done any of the things people do when they desire someone else. My body still reverberating with electrical energy, I gave my speech which received a standing ovation – Camilla clapping loudest of all.

Afterwards, I was incapable of hiding away as before and went along to the hotel bar with my fellow attendees. I found myself seeking Camilla almost constantly and each time our eyes met, her gaze penetrated through all of my defences, straight into my heart. No, that's not quite right. It was deeper than that – straight into my *soul*.

By the time most delegates were heading to bed, I had drunk five large gin and tonics and my resolve not to get involved with this woman had weakened considerably. When she finally sat next to me, I could not resist touching her knee with my own and within a few moments, we were covertly linking little fingers under the table… and the tingling recommenced. I imbibed yet another beverage, and when she said, 'Would you like to join me in my room for a nightcap?', I had no defences left. I was on fire!

She kissed me as soon as her door swung shut. And it was a kiss like no other. Although I had made love with dozens of men and women in my eighty years on this mortal coil, never had I experienced anything quite so extraordinary. It was like a visitation from God or perhaps I should say, the Goddess. Rapturous and terrifying in equal measure. I became lost in an ocean of ecstasy, a veritable sea of love – every cell in my body feeling as though it were healing as a consequence of our union.

I wish I could to tell you that I then accepted this unique and spiritual connection. A profound love to be prized above all others – a gift so precious that I grasped onto it with both hands – in spite of my many reservations. But alas, I did not… Rather, after hours of blissful love-making, once Camilla had fallen asleep in my arms, I gently extracted myself, silently dressed and then tiptoed away.

I did not even attempt to go to bed. Instead, I packed my suitcase, called a taxi to the station and left on the first train back to London.

As the train forged ahead in the direction of home, I tried to make sense of what had occurred. Why was this feeling, this experience, this particular instance of falling in love, so different from when I fell deeply in love with Abigail or Sebastian? How could someone so totally wrong, feel so absolutely right?

On reaching my house, I went to bed immediately, exhausted by all that had transpired and still unable to truly comprehend it. But my dreams were full of Camilla and our love-making, and when I awoke three hours later, I was yet more distressed.

I staggered downstairs to check my emails – already knowing she would have contacted me. She was, in fact, somewhat guarded in her words. She did not chastise me for leaving without saying goodbye, but instead, affirmed I was the most intelligent, impressive and inspiring human being she had ever encountered, and what a privilege it was to hear me speak and spend such wonderful personal time with me. She then stated she would be in London in two weeks time and asked if we could meet for dinner, signing off with the phrase, 'Love and best wishes, Camilla'.

I emailed back immediately, telling her I'd had a fabulous time at the conference and wishing her best of luck for the future but was unable to meet for dinner because I would be overseas by then. Which was a downright lie. In spite of all that we had shared, the passion, the bliss, the elation, I was unable to write what I actually felt which was, 'I have fallen hopelessly in love with you and all I want is to utterly lose myself in you for all eternity. Please come to me forthwith and never leave my side again.' I could not even get as far as, 'Please do join me for afternoon tea when you are next in London.'

She replied a few hours later, to say she was sorry that I was away when she was in London but to please let her know when I was back, as she would love to see me again. This time signing off with, 'Much love'.

I did not respond. I decided it better to retreat. But although we were now separated by two hundred miles, I continued to feel our connection. It was still resonating throughout my body, through my very soul, irrespective of the physical distance. It was so bizarre that I did not even know whether to believe it were real or whether I was becoming fanciful in my old age. After all, I barely believed in God, let alone the concept of spiritual connections.

Yet I was determined not to relent and decided I would only answer emails concerning professional matters. I was not going to come out at the age of eighty. Besides, even if she agreed to a secret relationship, being spotted more than once with someone so obviously lesbian, would first arouse suspicion and then ultimately lead to a scandal from which I might never recover. I had grandchildren to consider after all. What might happen to their prospects were it to get out that Grandma'ma was embroiled in a Sapphic relationship with a middle class doctor from the North?

As time went on, Camilla must have become frustrated with the lack of progress, as she invited me to more and more medical events, all of which I refused. Not because I didn't want to go, didn't want to see her, but because I knew that were I to see her, I would not be able to resist falling into her arms once again. Sometimes, I came close to attending an event anyway, even if I'd refused her invitation. One day, I even found myself putting on my make-up and moving towards the coat stand, before stopping myself from going to her.

And then, a few months later, the inevitable happened. I attended a day conference where I had no expectation of seeing her but there she was across the room. As soon as our eyes met, I felt myself fall yet more deeply in love. Suddenly she was no longer a forbidden fantasy. She was there before me.

In the first break, she came over to me and as we embraced, my body began to quiver. But I pretended I felt nothing, experienced nothing, wanted nothing. She behaved as though our relationship was perfectly normal and chatted about the conference and her work, and asked about mine. In spite of the underlying sexual tension, there was still an ease with which we communicated – a natural flow from a shared way of looking at the world and common sense of humour. Then as the conference recommenced, we returned to our seats like two people who just happened to know one another, rather than two beings who were madly in love.

At luncheon, we were seated at opposite ends of the banquet hall, but all I had to do was glance in her direction and, as before, she would sense it and gaze back. Then in the afternoon, I popped out to the ladies during a long and somewhat uninspiring lecture on new methods of treating pancreatitis, and as I was washing my hands, Camilla appeared through the door…

It was I who pulled her into the cubicle. We made love standing up in silence – so still, there was barely a rustle from our clothes. The kind of love-making I'd indulged in on countless occasions whilst at boarding school. Furtive, exhilarating and perilous. The euphoria making me feel like a teenager again. Afterwards, when she went to speak, I pressed my finger to her lips, hearing the main door opening as someone else entered. When the nearby cubicle door swung shut, I extracted myself from her embrace, indicating I would leave first. Then I flushed the toilet and opened the door, leaving her to gently push it closed after me. As soon as we were parted, I found myself rushing to the exit and marching to the station without looking back.

By the time I was at my desk, there was a fresh email from Camilla, begging me to call her. But I did not dare. If she had my phone number, even if I staved her off this time, I might not maintain my resolve in the future. I had to hold my nerve. I had been reckless. I had been unfair. There was no way I was going to have a relationship with this woman. So I simply ignored her. And all subsequent emails, professional or otherwise, until they stopped.

I won't tire you by recounting the four other occasions a similar scenario unfolded. We would be thrown together at a conference, end up making love in a ladies cloakroom and then I would run away and ignore all ensuing communication. But nonetheless, I was still consumed by her. Indeed, I believed I felt her with me constantly – on some other plane or energetic frequency. As though we were having a relationship anyway, irrespective of my best efforts to defy it.

I should have known that eventually one of us would crack. After over two years of this agonising preternatural union, interspersed with the occasional dose of real world clandestine lovemaking, I received an old fashioned letter through the post. In it, she said that life was too short and she could no longer settle for unplanned illicit encounters. She declared she was in love with me and that she believed I felt the same way about her, and that she wanted to meet so we could talk properly about our extraordinary connection.

I spent the next two weeks in a state of abject catatonia. Barely able eat or sleep. Part of me wanted to pick up the phone, confess I was madly in love with her and ask her to come to me. But the other half of me was utterly horrified to see her words of love laid bare.

Finally after a fortnight had passed, I realised I had a moral duty to at least respond in some manner. I could not write that I was not in love with her. I simply could not. But in spite of the magnitude of my own feelings, I was still not prepared to relent. And so I wrote the vaguest reply possible but one that I knew would end all further correspondence on the matter. It said, 'I am sorry you feel so strongly about me. But I am not in a position to even countenance a relationship. Kind regards, Lucinda.'

As anticipated, I did not receive another letter. And though my heart shattered into a thousand shards, I did not acquiesce and reach for her. Instead I decided to stop attending medical conferences altogether. After all, I was eighty-two now – it wasn't as though I was obliged.

[LUCINDA PAUSES LOOKING SAD]

I was aware of Camilla in spirit for nearly another year. However, in time, the feeling became intermittent until, eventually, her energetic presence diminished altogether. And I knew, simply knew, she had met someone else… And, as a consequence, I became deeply lonely and consumed by regret.

[LUCINDA PAUSES AND, USING A SILK HANDKERCHIEF, WIPES AWAY A TEAR.]

A few months on, now over three years since we had fallen in love, I finally saw Camilla once again. We were both attending a garden party hosted by an establishment peer, well known for making significant donations to medical institutions. She was accompanied by a woman who I instantly knew was her lover and it utterly crippled me. The agony in my heart and solar plexus at seeing her happy with another, was so excruciating, I could barely find my breath.

As Camilla's new partner was swept away by a group of medics, I found myself walking towards her, finally wishing to discuss all that had passed between us. When I reached her, Camilla smiled but despite her welcoming demeanour, there was pain in her eyes. Filled with remorse and longing for her love, I told her I was sorry that I hadn't been able to give her what she wanted but I was happy that she had met someone who clearly had. Which was, of course, an outright falsehood because I was now going out of my mind with jealousy.

She said, ‘Thank you,’ and started to leave, but spontaneously I grabbed her arm and the pain in her eyes increased tenfold. Suddenly I heard myself saying, ‘I love you!’ even though I had vowed never to declare it. She looked at me in disdain, giving an indignant laugh. ‘I *know* you do. But that was never the problem, was it? The problem was you didn’t *want* to. It was easier for you to break your own heart and deny our connection, than have any kind of relationship with me!’

I tried to assert again that it was because I knew I could not give her what she wanted, at which point she became so furious with me, she almost drew attention to us. ‘You never even asked what I wanted, you simply assumed. I mean, did you really think I’d to force you to come out, set up house and get a cat? I was sixty-two for heaven’s sake, not twenty-two. I really wasn't dreaming of a white picket fence!’

On this, she marched away in the direction of her new girlfriend, and I was forced to slip out of the event and take the long way back to the station via the park, lest I be spotted weeping by someone I knew.

As I walked, I contemplated what Camilla had said about expectations, and realised that I had indeed made unfounded assumptions. Her eyes had been wide open about the limitations of any long-term union between us but she had wanted me anyway. Loved me anyway. Remained patient – too patient for her own good –

while I had stubbornly resisted her, only to now find myself thoroughly inconsolable.

I then took a long hard look at myself. As an intelligent, exceptionally well-educated and brilliant, successful surgeon, one would think I could have found a way to have a love life that was completely open and on my own terms. But no! For my entire existence, I had remained ensnared by the rules of People Like Us. I had demanded no more emotional freedom than those girls whom I had looked down on for settling for a life of purchasing just the right antiques and organising soirees.

I found myself wringing my hands in despair. Why did I just accept that Abigail and I could have no future? Why did I stop sleeping with Leona even though we were having a wonderful time – when my husband continued on sleeping with *his* secretary unfettered? Why, after he passed away, did I never consider even asking any of my subsequent female lovers to have a more formal relationship? And why, oh why, when I had found such true love, such a pure love with Camilla, had I thrown it away? Suddenly I wanted to run to her… but I knew it was far too late. Even if she still had feelings, she would never trust me now. She would not relinquish her new lover to take another chance on me. I had lost her and I had only myself to blame.

[LUCINDA PAUSES, WIPING AWAY ANOTHER TEAR.]

They were married this morning – Camilla and her partner Loran. There is no happy ever after for me. I will go to my grave knowing that I could have been deliriously happy until the day I died, were it not for my own intransigence. And I am furious with myself for not being more courageous. For conforming. And, of course, for hurting *her* so much.

So, as of *this* day – the day when I have had to accept the heartbreaking ramifications of my own actions – I have decided to at last be brave, break ranks, overturn convention and openly admit to the world – *my* world – who I am. I will never pretend or deny it again. I shall finally say it. I shall even shout it from the rooftops. For perhaps, this will help someone else from my set not to make the same egregious mistakes as I, break the cycle, and end this ridiculous charade performed by People Like Us.

My name is Lucinda and I am bisexual.

Monologue 4.

Footballer's Wife

[LAURA IS SITTING IN A LARGE BACK GARDEN WITH A HUGE LAWN. SHE IS WEARING GOOD QUALITY GREY COTTON CARGO TROUSERS AND A CHECKED GREY AND PINK BRUSHED COTTON BLOUSE. HER HAIR IS TIED BACK IN A BUN AND HER MAKE-UP IS PERFECT. AS SHE TELLS HER STORY, VARIOUS DOGS OF DIFFERENT SHAPES AND SIZES COME IN AND OUT OF VIEW. SHE SPEAKS WITH RECEIVED PRONUNCIATION BUT OCCASIONALLY, HER NATURAL BIRMINGHAM ACCENT SEEPS THROUGH.]

By the time I reached the ripe old age of eighty, I had lived exactly half of my life without human company, instead preferring to cohabit with dogs. On the day my life changed beyond all comprehension, I had a pack of seventeen canines, each of whom I had rescued in one way or another. At times, the total had risen beyond that, but a dog's life is short so numbers fluctuated over the years.

On the day in question, I'd had a fairly ordinary morning by my standards. All dogs capable of walking had been taken to the beach for an hour. Those who could not walk far had then been wheeled along the prom in an oversized pram so they'd get a change of scenery. Seventeen varying sized breakfasts had been served and one of my oldest dogs, Jasper, had been taken to the vets to be examined because a lump had formed on his chest. Nothing unusual in the daily life of a 'mad dog lady'.

That afternoon, however, there was an unexpected, frantic knocking on my door, which sent my dogs into a collective frenzy. Once I had sufficiently calmed down the rabble of multifarious barking canines, I finally managed to get through the dog-gate in the hallway and open the door – only to be greeted by a distressed young woman with short straggly blonde hair, a face running with mascara, wearing a cheap looking dress that did nothing to hide two bandaged wrists.

Much to my shock, the distraught teenager threw herself into my arms crying, 'Granny, don't you recognise me? It's me – Jo!' I pulled back as much as I could from the unfamiliar looking girl and finally realised that it was my youngest grandchild who I had not seen in two years. And this is when the most important part of my life's journey began. A journey which is by no means over yet, perhaps not even halfway through, but one which was foretold more than six decades ago.

Let me explain from the beginning… In the summer of 1951, having not long turned sixteen and just left school for good, I went with my family on our annual day trip to Blackpool. This was the nearest thing to a holiday we ever had, and this year, my special treat when we arrived in this magical paradise by the sea, was my mother taking me to see the fortune-teller on the North Pier. When the wizened old gypsy woman examined my right palm, she raised her eyebrows, giving me a twinkly smile. 'Well!' she said. 'This is one of the most interesting hands I've read in a very long time!' I smiled back, excited to know more but she paused before speaking further and stared into her crystal ball. 'Yes, the crystal confirms it. I see you having a long, long life. I see you still standing at one hundred years old. I see you marrying a poor man who becomes rich. You will know luxury and fortune that you did not dream possible. But you will also know great sorrow, and it will not be until the last quarter of your life that you will understand why you were born and what your purpose is.'

I remember leaving the psychic's tacky little booth feeling utterly exhilarated. After all, no girl who grew up in the abject poverty of the back to back houses in Birmingham was going to turn her nose up at the possibility of being wealthy and leading a lavish life!

That was the only time I ever visited a clairvoyant. I know some people go regularly but the gypsy's reading was so powerful, I never felt the need. And besides, unlikely though it may sound to you, one way or another, everything she predicted that day did, in fact, come to pass.

[LAURA PAUSES]

I need to tell you a bit more about my past – so you understand my life – and how fate took me on this journey like no other.

As I mentioned, I grew up poor. A working class girl from a family that had been lucky to survive the vagaries of inner city life – long freezing winters with barely enough coal for a fire, parents who had both experienced being on the brink of starvation in their younger years, who then struggled to feed me and my five brothers – my dad's meagre wages as a brickie and mom's top up from taking in laundry, barely amounting to enough to keep the wolf from the door.

Being the only girl in a house full of sons, I had special status with my parents and even though they had nothing, I was still pampered and prettified compared to my brothers, who at times went to school in cut down wellington boots when shoes had worn out before money could be found to replace them.

In spite of the abject poverty in which we were raised, the one thing that my brothers had in their favour was they all loved football and the senior school they attended had a sports master in love with the 'beautiful game'. He made sure that all kit was provided by the school, so even the most destitute of boys had a chance to play on the team.

Because of being the only girl in a football mad family, right from the word go, I knew everything there was to know about tackling and passing, the off-side rule, and team formations. I spent so much time as a youngster standing on the sidelines of local pitches, witnessing both the agony and the ecstasy, that it was inevitable I would eventually become a Footballer's Wife.

We're not talking a 'WAG' here. Thank god, the rise of the WAG did not happen until my children were immersed in the sport. But nonetheless, the special status of 'wife of famous footballer' would soon become mine.

Bill, like me, grew up with nothing. A life where you got a bar of chocolate and a tangerine for Christmas… but like my brothers, he had been kicking a ball up and down the street since he could toddle, and eventually, like them, he had made the school team. But unlike my brothers, whose passion for the game only got them as far as the amateur league, Bill had that little something extra that changed both his destiny and mine, from a life of scarcity to one of abundance.

I'd always known Bill from a distance but about six weeks after the gypsy had told my fortune, he came over to me after a game and asked me whether I wanted to go to a dance. At this stage, I had no inkling that it would be *he* who would pull me from rags to riches. He was just a handsome lad with a cheeky smile who I liked the look of. I was now working as a shop assistant in the local haberdashery, having left school with a basic School Certificate and no expectations of continuing on. Bill, however, had stayed on to do the more advanced High School Certificate just so he could keep playing as part of the school football team because he loved it so much and the sports master was so brilliant.

We had a very ordinary courtship – me standing on the sidelines, cheering him on at games, lots of outings to the pictures and occasionally going to a dance. I hadn't really had a sweetheart before, other than the occasional kiss behind the big oak tree at the local park with a boy who lived down the road. But Bill was different. We courted for over year and then, when he was still seventeen years old, he was spotted by a talent scout and snapped up by a professional club. That night he asked me to marry him and I said, 'Yes,' straight away.

I was excited for him and for me. He would have a good wage as a professional footballer and because he was always in training, he didn't drink that much compared to his peers – so he seemed like a man who could provide me with a brilliant and beautiful future.

How in love with him I actually was, I really do not know. But Bill certainly made my heart flutter and made me dream of an idyllic life that only a teenager could fantasise as being possible. And after all, maybe the gypsy was right. Could this be the poor man who would become rich? He certainly wasn't destined for a life of scrimping and scraping – and that was about as fortunate as a girl from my background could get. So on my nineteenth birthday, with Bill by now a fully-fledged member of a first division squad, I married him.

I think I already inferred that I didn't have a career plan. I'd grown up with the expectation of working in a shop or a factory until I had babies and then doing whatever was necessary to top up the income of my husband. But by the time we married, Bill was already earning more than enough for me to give up my job immediately, and instead, a new set of expectations came my way – namely, to negotiate without training, how to be the wife of a man whose fame and earnings rose exponentially each year, and how to climb socially at the same rate.

For suddenly, we were living a life of home ownership, formal dinners in expensive restaurants, and soirees in five star hotels. We were still children really, with no idea about etiquette, and it became clear within a few months of Bill's rise to fame, that we were going to have to learn our new world so we didn't keep making the mistakes of people who were raised dirt poor – such as wearing the wrong attire to important events, not knowing which knives and forks were used in a five course meal, buying expensive purchases that actually looked tacky in the eyes of those who came from more affluent backgrounds.

The pressure on both of us, and consequently our marriage, was enormous. It was after about a year, when our honeymoon period wore off, that the rot set in. Bill had always had a temper but until then, had contained it to noisy ranting after matches where he had missed an important goal. But then one evening, after what can only be described as a disastrous dinner party which I'd held for the team in our brand new house, Bill's temper took an unexpected turn that started a downward spiral from which we would never recover.

Nothing I had cooked turned out well, and unsubtle comments were made about our lack of taste in crockery. When the door was closed on the final guest, Bill, who'd consumed three times more alcohol than normal in order to deal with the mortification caused by *my* failure, went into the kitchen and smashed every single cup, plate and dish against the wall – ranting all the while about my uselessness as a wife, and listing an array of faults, including ones I did not even know I had.

I had never witnessed a display of such unfettered anger before. My father had been firm but fair with us, and only ever raised a hand if we did something so dangerous that the slap would be shock enough for us never to do it again. But this was something altogether different. A rage so ferocious it had a life of its own –

determined to destroy everything in its path. I was absolutely terrified.

I do not need to tell you that this was the first of many such incidents and episodes, and that of course, eventually, it wasn't just the china that got broken.
Once the genie was out of the bottle, there was no putting it back and I became one of so many women of my generation, and indeed yours, who found themselves married to a monster and unable to find a way out. There were few refuges for women like me in the 1950s and 60s. And there was no point calling the police because they didn't deal back then with what were referred to as 'domestic rows'. I was alone. My family and friends were oblivious to my ordeal, believing I was the luckiest woman on the planet. And as I withdrew into my shell, instead of asking me if I was alright, they started thinking I was ashamed of them and had become a snob.

I soon realised that to get through this existence with minimal beatings, I could not afford to make even the tiniest mistake. I had to find a way to remain faultless. So I turned my attention to becoming the perfect Footballer's Wife. I may not have had much of an education but I wasn't stupid, and I knew I needed to school myself in every aspect of being the *impeccable* woman with the *impeccable* home. So I read every book I could find on good housekeeping and furniture magazines galore, so my husband would never hear ridicule about his home or its contents again.

I also studied the wives of the middle class players who seemed to execute the myriad expectations of their role as Footballer's Wife so effortlessly. They moved, dressed and spoke completely differently from me. So I went to several classes to learn comportment and found myself a fashion consultant to help me choose clothes that were classy as well as stylish. I realised I had to look glamorous enough at all times so every man would want me, but never dress in a way that would suggest *I* might want them. One slip into looking slutty or cheap might mean a week nursing a sprained wrist or a bruised back.

I also noticed that when we were not in the Midlands, people smirked at and sometimes even imitated my accent for a laugh. And therefore, I took elocution lessons so I no longer sounded like a Brummy, and extended my vocabulary so I could use big words in the right way.

[LAURA THEN SPEAKS IN A STRONG BIRMINGHAM ACCENT]

Can yow believe I used to talk like this?!

[LAURA PAUSES]

The more faultlessly I presented myself to the wider world and the fewer mistakes I made, the more chance I had of getting through the aftermath of a bad game without a black eye – although this was never guaranteed. Sometimes I only had to look at Bill with the wrong expression and he would hit me.

As a consequence, make-up became my obsession – covering bruises with foundation, eye shadow and powder, became my art. Within three years of being married, there was not a single brand of make up in Great Britain that I had not tried and tested. I had mastered every technique available – there was no injury I could not cover or camouflage. I was an expert.

[LAURA PAUSES AND LOOKS SERIOUS]

Not all women who know about make-up do so because they are vain. Just remember that, please. It's so easy to make assumptions about women who are all glammed up. But for some women, it is the means to their very survival…
I mean, can you imagine what Bill might have done to me had someone noticed one of the bruises on my face and asked a probing question…?

[LAURA PAUSES AGAIN]

Anyway, it wasn't long before the excruciating loneliness of being a Footballer's Wife became completely entrenched and the material wealth surrounding me provided cold comfort. I'd love to be able to tell you that having children gave me great solace and made my marriage bearable. But having our first son, Mark, did nothing to make Bill tender again. It was made very clear that rearing the children was solely my responsibility so he could focus on his game. However, although I wanted to be the best, gentlest, kindest mother possible, it was also made clear that no son of Bill's was to be 'namby pambied'. He needed to grow up ready to be a footballer himself and that meant being hard. If Mark cried in the night and I cuddled him for too long, I would be criticised for making him soft. If I gave him a teddy bear, I would be told off for turning him into a 'poofter'. Any maternal affection or reaction had to be mitigated when Bill was home, and he insisted Mark go to a nursery as soon as he was weaned because he didn't want him to be a 'mummy's boy'.

The arrival of our second son, James, a year and a half later did nothing to change Bill's views on parenting. And by the time our third son, Andrew, came along, I was still only twenty-four years old and the period of great sorrow predicted by the gypsy had become what felt like a relentless, eternal existence that would simply never end. There were days when I felt suicidal, believing there would never again be a time when I might feel happiness for more than the length of a child's smile at being given a sweetie. I had no one to turn to. Nowhere to go. I was trapped in a gilded cage. But I knew I never would take my own life because remote though my parents and brothers had become, I could never bring upon them such shame and sorrow...

So instead, I slowly died inside until I became numb. I didn't even feel hurt or angry when Bill started having full-blown affairs with other women, rather than just putting it about. I had known he was philandering from early on in the marriage for he didn't even bother to hide the lipstick on his collar or the smell of cheap perfume on his tie. Sometimes he stayed out all night without explanation. And if he came near me, it wasn't an expression of love. I was now just a convenient, ever present receptacle. In fact, I took great relief when his women on the side were more serious than just a night, because it meant he was home less often and barely touched me.

As our sons grew up, Bill was yet more conscious of our 'New Money' status and determined that as well as them becoming footballers like him, they should also have every opportunity in life that he was denied because of poverty. Soon came the onslaught of boys' private schools and boys' football leagues and other extra curricular activities that snatched my children away from me almost completely. They didn't even come to me if they cut a knee, but instead had learned from their father 'to be a man', dress it themselves and play on. By the time my sons reached their teenage years, they saw me as nothing but a food dispenser and washerwoman. Their lives were firmly ensconced in the world of men. They had no more respect for women than Bill did, despite my best efforts to teach them otherwise.

I wish I could say that eventually, as the status of women grew stronger and the first seeds of feminism turned to green shoots, that I found the bravery to leave Bill. But in all honesty, I never worked out how. I mean – much as I felt distanced from our sons – our life was in the public eye, and as Bill continued straight from the field into management, there was no let up of interest in our family.

In the end, it was Bill who did the leaving. In 1975, the year we both turned forty, Bill told me he was in love with his personal assistant and wanted a divorce. I signed the papers without hesitation and finally escaped. Our older sons, Mark and James, were already professional footballers themselves and Andrew, aged sixteen, was heading towards the same fate. What little connection I had with them as a mother was so miniscule that when I moved out, the idea of them living with anyone other than their father was not even considered.

So I embarked on a new life. A better life. One where I was unafraid of the turn of the key in the door. I decided to move away from the Midlands altogether. My parents had both passed away whilst I was married, and my five brothers all worshipped Bill as the 'God of Football', and saw me as a failure for not holding down my marriage to this man so worthy of adulation. Surely him sleeping with his P.A. was *my* fault? I clearly had not been a good enough wife, not looked after myself enough, not revered him sufficiently as the deity he was. All my childhood friends were long gone and I'd not made any new ones because I could not be honest about the abject misery of my life – and so any connections had remained superficial. I was totally alone.

The only thing I had in my favour was enough money from the divorce settlement to buy a house outright. And I decided then I would come and live in this marvellous place – Blackpool – the only place I had ever associated with absolute happiness and joy. Funfairs, trams, slot machines, cabaret shows, twinkly lights, sticks of rock and candyfloss. The best times of my childhood had been spent here in this tacky working class heaven called Blackpool, and I'd even managed to sneak my sons here once when they were small and Bill was away with the team.

I found myself a house with a sea and Blackpool Tower view, and decided I needed a new purpose so bought myself a golden retriever puppy called Jess. Bill had never let me have a dog. He hated them with a passion, and I knew if I brought one into the house against his will, he would abuse it as much as me, so I had resisted. Now, the new autonomous me decided to finally live on my own terms and have something *I* wanted.

There are miles of golden sands in Blackpool. A broken woman with a puppy can find great solace in a long, bracing walk to the never quite fading accompaniment of music from amusement arcades and fairground rides.

And soon one puppy became two and then a third dog found wandering along the beach became three, and then the old lady next door dying suddenly meant four. And a growing passion for taking in waifs and strays began and my pack expanded year on year.

I did not marry again. I tried dating a few times after the divorce, but whenever a man showed even the slightest bit of anger or frustration, I found myself quivering and wondering when that anger would be turned on me. Eventually, I realised that I could never and would never trust a man again and instead, I concentrated on my dogs.

By the time I was eighty, the prediction from the fortune-teller about the last part of my life being the most important, actually felt like it had already come true in a funny kind of way. Mainly because of the number of dogs I'd rescued in the forty years between divorcing Bill and my youngest grandchild turning up unexpectedly on my doorstep. But in fact, this period was still to come.

[LAURA PAUSES]

Jo was the youngest child of my youngest child, Andrew, who'd been sixteen years old when Bill and I divorced, and who I'd only seen on high days and holidays ever since.

In fact, as a consequence of moving here, I'd barely spent any time with any of my three sons or their children. They'd been sucked into that world of football as Bill had, and I would not attend family events if Bill was going to be there. I was regarded by my grandchildren as the 'mad grandma up north' who cared more about stray dogs than her own family.

But that afternoon, when the weeping teenager crossed the threshold of my home, battered and suicidal – in spite of my shock and difficulty in understanding what had befallen me – I embraced her. I say 'shock' because it was.... For the last time I had seen Jo, she had been my youngest grand*son*, not my grand*daughter*. She had been born a boy.

I needn't tell you why she had been forced to flee. A transgender child in any family is lucky to reach adolescence without a dozen scars on each arm. But in a footballing family, and a famous one at that, what chance did a girl trapped inside a boy's body have to navigate her perilous journey? So whatever my initial shock and reaction to this revelation was, and in spite of my ignorance back then regarding all thing trans, I knew immediately that I was the only thing standing between Jo and an early grave. That if *I* didn't help, if *I* didn't accept, if *I* didn't support this girl – this sixteen year old *girl*, whose life had been one of torture since infancy – then *I* would have as much blood on my hands as my son would.

I'd love to be able to tell you that I accepted Jo as a trans girl straight away. But I didn't. I'm not a hero. I'm not the ultimate 'tranny granny' who just lovingly scooped up her dysphoric grandchild and made everything alright. When I let her across the threshold and into my life, I was as much disturbed as I was repelled. I won't lie to you about that. I'd seen plenty of drag queens walking into the famous cabaret bars we have here in Blackpool, but I'd never, to my knowledge, met a trans person before – and at eighty, my ideas about such people were imbued with a disgust and an obtuseness typical of someone of my generation. But even though at this stage my emotional connection to Jo was miniscule compared to so many grandparents with their grandchildren, I still felt the pull and protectiveness that comes with family blood.

After she had cried in my arms for over an hour, Jo told me of the hideousity of her life. Her father thinking she was a 'poof' from an early age, making her do more and more sport to 'make a man of her', and beating her every time any hint of femininity emerged. Her mother, treating her with repulsion – having caught Jo on too many occasions dressing up in her clothes – threatening 'to tell Dad', threatening to send her to boarding school, threatening to send her to the 'loony bin'.

I asked all sorts of what now seem stupid questions – which at the time felt perfectly logical – like how did she know she was a woman rather than a gay man? And how did she know she wasn't a drag queen or a transvestite? But as the conversation unfolded, I realised that this sixteen year old child needed to be a woman, even if it was just for now, if she was going to make it through the night and then the next week and the week after that. So I looked her up and down and said, 'Well if you insist on being a woman, you should at least know how to do your make-up properly!' And I took her by the hand and led her across a room full of somewhat inquisitive dogs, up the stairs to my vanity unit, where I pulled out my cleanser and studied her face. And then, once she was a blank canvas, began to apply foundation and product after product, until she did indeed look like a real girl, rather than a boy just dressing up.

Seeing herself as she really could be for the very first time, made her cry so much that the new make-up barely lasted five minutes. But I knew without question that I had saved my grandchild's life that evening.

Ironically, although I still wore make-up every day, I had very few clothes I could give to Jo, because I had for years by then, been dressing in the standard utilitarian trousers and shirts necessary to live successfully as a 'crazy dog rescuer'. But I pulled out a couple of skirts and blouses, and took her to the spare bedroom and put them in the wardrobe. And said, 'We'll get you some more clothes tomorrow. This is *your* room now. You can decorate it however you want.'

'Can I really stay here?' she asked me timidly. I fought off my – what now could be described as – ingrained 'transphobia' and smiled and replied, 'Yes. So long as you pay your way by helping me with all aspects of looking after the dogs. I was thinking about getting a helper anyway.'

The look of relief on her face was so overwhelming that I shed a tear. She said she'd always wanted a dog and she'd love to know how to care for them the way I did, so I replied, 'Well, now you have seventeen!' Then I went downstairs to give the dogs their evening meal, and Jo followed and helped.

And so our life together began…

As it was, although Jo had not had a chance to manifest as a woman on the outside – apart from a few snatched stealthy moments – she knew so much about who she was because of the internet. It had been finding secret forums for girls like her that had enabled her to survive as long as she had.

But it was little wonder that on her sixteenth birthday, she'd run away and come to me. That morning, now she was an adult, Jo had bought some girls' clothes and dressed up to show her parents who she really was – only to be beaten and berated. So she'd then taken a chance and got on a train to Blackpool – because I was the only person she could think of who might let her through the door. And I probably was.

When I phoned Andrew, a bit later, to let him know Jo was with me, he asked me if Jo was dressed as a girl, and I said, 'Yes'. He did nothing but hurl abuse at me for letting Jo into my home dressed like that, and told me he would never speak to me again if I allowed Jo to live with me as a girl. I said that I would let Jo live with me any way *Jo* saw fit, then slammed the phone down – hating him in that moment, almost as much as I hated his father.

I know that in these liberated days, there are some parents who allow their children to manifest as they feel naturally inclined, and this must take the pressure off those vulnerable, delicate children – but even then, their path is not easy to follow. However Jo, like many other trans children, had spent her sixteen years as a girl trapped in a boy's body, living an existence of fear that was similar to the one I had lived in when married to Bill. Always trying hard to get it right and paying for the smallest mistake with a black eye or a sprained arm. My son, Andrew, was nothing short of a carbon copy of his father. I had never really gotten to know his wife, but from what Jo told me, Andrew's fists were not solely reserved for his children. So I do wonder whether she took his side partly for her own survival. Whatever the case, Jo did not stand a chance of surviving, let alone thriving, in that environment any longer than she did. I still think it's a miracle that she made it to her sixteenth birthday.

[LAURA PAUSES, KNITTING HER EYEBROWS TOGETHER FOR A MOMENT]

What I am about to say might not sit well with some people, but I need to say I was relieved that Jo could not start taking hormones until she was eighteen. I firmly believe she needed to fully know not just what it was like to dress and look like a woman, but also to actually *live* as a woman before taking the steps that would change her body.

I don't care what anyone says, becoming a woman instead of being a man, means giving up a huge amount of power and status. Even the most effeminate man will largely be given more respect in society than most women are. And I wanted Jo to be sure she could cope with living as a second class citizen for the rest of her life – especially as even after hormones and surgery, it might still be possible for people to tell that she was trans. So I was glad she had two years where she worked out for sure who she was – whether she was indeed a woman, rather than an effeminate man who could not bear the strain of masculine expectations.

She decided to keep the name Jo – she had always gone by it, having been christened Joseph. Many trans folk shed their birth name but she didn't feel it necessary. 'Jo for Josephine' was fine by her. And so, one of the first things we did was change her name by deed poll. A relatively easy thing to change back if she had made a mistake, but a monumental landmark moment for

Josephine in becoming the woman she was so certain she was.

We also went to the doctor, and eventually, after what seemed like an age, she was referred to a clinic. Then, after countless sessions of counselling, she was formally diagnosed with ‘gender dysphoria’, which meant she could be put on the list to start physically transitioning, once she had turned eighteen.

And then we set out to make friends. Jo and me together. We found every group and support network, and we even sneaked her into nightclubs. One of the wonderful things about Blackpool is that there really is something for everyone, and on our doorstep was a world that I had previously not known existed – but a world which would become vital to both *her* mental health and *my* understanding.

I also made her find a part-time job in one of the many seaside gift shops we have here, so she would be forced to interact as a woman with countless people from all over the country, and be prepared for the array of reactions she might get.

By the time Jo reached eighteen, she had lived successfully and happily as a young woman for two years. She knew nearly every drag queen, transvestite and trans woman living in and around Blackpool. She had spoken to everyone, asked every possible question and had watched as new friends, older than her, had begun the long drawn out process of gender reassignment, and had made sure she understood both the wonderful and challenging things that lay ahead. And she was absolutely certain it was right for her to transition fully. And actually, by then, so was I. But the rest of our family were not…

On the morning of her eighteenth birthday, we were woken up at six o'clock by the racket of, now nineteen dogs, barking agitatedly at a thunderous pounding on the front door. Somehow, in the chaos, I managed to get them all behind the hall dog-gate and opened the door, only to find Bill, Andrew, his wife Monica, Mark and James all standing angrily at my threshold. I had not seen Bill in over forty years, but even though he was now old and bent, fear rushed through me at the furious expression on his face, and I found myself gripping the door handle in case I needed to shut it. The dogs, knowing these were not friendly beings, were becoming more and more frantic and as I looked back I saw Jo, standing shuddering behind them, only visible to the aggressors on the doorstep as a shadow.

It was Andrew who spoke first. 'Jeremy tells us his brother is going to turn into a girl today and we've driven through the night to put a stop to it. We've been hearing all sorts over the last two years but we haven't come up here earlier because we hoped it was just a teenage fad – given that being *transexual* is all the rage right now. But there's no way my son is turning into a girl. I'm here to take him home.'

Terrified, I paused for a moment and then, still scared that I might come to physical harm, did something that in my forty years as a dog owner, I had never even countenanced. I took a step back, reached over for my German Shepherd Rex's collar, swiftly opened the dog-gate, and brought him out by my side. And together, we stepped forward. On seeing the dog, whose teeth were now bared, the rabble of angry relatives collectively moved back. I then knew that I had gained enough control of the situation for no one to even attempt either hitting me or dragging Jo from her home.

I took a deep breath and then finally addressed them. 'Jo is *not* turning into a girl today. Jo has *always* been a girl. She is eighteen years old and has lived as the woman she is for two years. So there is absolutely nothing you can do legally to prevent her from taking the medical steps necessary to become the person she already is on the inside, on the outside too.'

At this, Bill, unfettered by age, started to rant, calling me a 'twisted old bitch' who was only doing this to get revenge on *him* for marrying a younger woman, and on *Andrew* for wanting to stay with him instead of me once we were divorced. What Bill didn't notice, as he ranted and raged, was the number of trans women, drag queens, lesbians and gay men who were approaching – each recording him on their phones. Jo had clearly put out an urgent call on social media for her friends to come and help, and they had done so.

It was only when our family were finally surrounded from behind by an arc of twenty of Blackpool's finest, that Jo finally stepped out from behind the dogs – from the shadows and into the light, as the proud woman she had become. She silenced her grandfather and waited for a moment for the expressions of shock and disgust to abate, and then indicated to her father, mother, grandfather and uncles that they were very much surrounded and on camera. The look of horror on all of their faces was priceless. After all, four retired professional footballers being filmed ranting hatred and bile was sure to be a scandal that would hit the tabloids and go on for weeks. How could they even hope to endure it? And what would it do to those sons who'd carried on the family tradition and were now at the height of their footballing fame?

Once it was clear who now had the power, Jo turned to the LGBTQ crowd and said, 'Friends, thank you for coming to assist me. Please stop recording for the moment but leave your finger at the ready, in case it is required.' At which there was a collective nod. She then turned her attention to her parents. 'Mum, Dad. You've never accepted me. Never given me a chance to be who I am – not even a chance to *talk* about what has been going on inside of me since I was a toddler. And I simply could not be who or what you wanted. I have spent the last two years finally being able to breathe. Finally being able to embrace who I am, and finally being loved for who I am by the most caring, supportive and nurturing person I have ever known. Apart from Jeremy, none of you have even attempted to contact me, tell me you love me, or show any kind of care. You disowned me just because I tried to show you my true self. So how dare you come here today to try and stop me from doing what is within my legal and medical rights.' Jo paused then, took a deep breath, and then said in a clear, firm voice. 'And so now, *I* disown *you.* You are *not* my family. This woman standing next to me, and these people standing behind you are my *true* family. You just happen to be related to me by blood.'

She waited for a moment to let them fully absorb her words before finally addressing them again. 'Today,' she said, proudly, 'Is not only my eighteenth birthday. It is also my *liberation* day. The day I finally liberate myself from you and the day I begin my physical journey into womanhood. At four o'clock this afternoon, I will have my first injection of oestrogen and begin saying goodbye to this prison of a body, and feel it gradually becoming a loving home. And there's nothing *you* can do to prevent it. So do yourselves, Granny, me and these lovely people behind you a favour, and FUCK OFF AND DON'T COME BACK! We don't want you and we don't need you!'

At which point, now quivering a little, Jo turned on her heel and went back indoors, as the crowd behind gave a resounding cheer. I looked at each of my sons and then at Bill, shaking my head. 'You should be ashamed of yourselves,' I said flatly, before turning with my still snarling German Shepherd, and slamming the front door behind me.

[LAURA PAUSES AGAIN.]

That was three years ago and I am now eighty-five…

After three years of hormones, and five years of living as a woman, today, Jo took the final step in becoming the person she is. This morning, she underwent surgery to turn her penis inside out to become a working vagina.

I cannot tell you that it is a journey I have found easy in any way. I have worked through over eighty years of prejudice to get to the point where I can tell you my story today, without flinching or being ashamed. But I do know this. I love my grandchild. My granddaughter. And I know for sure she is female. And I know for sure that she deserves to live a happy life being as fully herself as she can be, given the hand she was dealt. And no one, absolutely no one, should be standing in her way of having that – whatever their feelings of discomfort.

I only hope that the clairvoyant, all those years ago, was right and I'll live until I'm at least a hundred. That way, I can continue to love and protect my most precious grandchild and give her a safe haven, no matter what the vicissitudes of life bring her way. And I hope that by the time I do die, the world will be a kinder, gentler, more understanding place for women like her. A world where she can walk down any street, anywhere and nobody takes a second glance. But in the meantime, I will keep fighting for her right to have that.

And also, before I go, I want to say this… because it might be my only chance. If you're one of those people who think that trans women are not real women, then let me tell you this... I lived in predominantly male environments for the first half of my life, and there is one thing I am absolutely certain of. One thing I know beyond any doubt. No *man* would ever choose to have his balls popped or his dick turned inside out! Even a top class footballer, would rather lose a leg than his cock! SO JUST STOP IT. STOP IT, WILL YOU. ENOUGH IS ENOUGH. TRANS WOMEN *ARE* WOMEN. END OF STORY.

About The Author

Rachel Dax is a Writer, Filmmaker and University Lecturer based in South Wales. Rachel is committed to writing original stories about LGBTQ characters and women who have been written out of history. She is the author of lesbian love story *After The Night* and genderqueer historical trilogy *The Legend Of Pope Joan*. Rachel has made several short films which have been screened across the globe. Her most recent film *Time & Again*, starring Dame Siân Phillips and Brigit Forsyth, has been shown at more than fifty festivals and won thirteen awards. *Time & Again* is currently available to watch on BBC iPlayer.

Rachel's main passions in life are Film, Theatre, Classical Music, Walking and Dogs.

Website www.daxitales.com
Email: info@daxitales.com

Printed in Poland
by Amazon Fulfillment
Poland Sp. z o.o., Wrocław